CRAZY AS ME

CRAZY AS ME

SASCHA MASETTO

Copyright © 2023 by Sascha Masetto

All rights reserved. No part of this book may be reproduced in any manner whatsoever without written permission except in the case of brief quotations embodied in critical articles and reviews.

First Printing, 2023

CHAPTER 1

Alvaro

"Come on, you can't be serious?"

Glen, my lawyer, peers over his thick glasses at me, giving away no emotion, no sympathy. I guess those are for his clients who actually pay on time. He crosses his skinny, pale arms across his chest, "Alvaro, not sure how many times we've been over this. You must leave the United States within thirty days of the end of your visa. The end of your visa was almost a year ago."

"We can't appeal?" I ask, knowing full well the answer, but hoping that the Federal Government of the United States of America has decided to change its entire immigration policy since I met with Glenn last Wednesday.

"What is there to appeal? You're out of time, Alvaro. You've been out of time. The lottery can't be re-entered, asylum spots from Mexico are full, you can't renew your visa without paying the school for tuition and, even still, you would have to leave the country to come back, which, of course, would alert the government of your unlawful presence, triggering a ban from re-entry. As I've said, **many times**, you have two options. Pay a million bucks for an investor visa or get married to an American citizen."

"And in the meantime?"

Glen shakes his head, "As your lawyer, I would strongly advise you to leave the country so as not to accrue any more unlawful presence here. The longer you're here, the longer the ban will be in the future."

"And as my friend, what do you advise?"

"You don't pay me to be your friend."

"Glenn," I make sure to say with desperation, channeling my inner actor. They say you should always use truth for a role, and I luckily have a lot to be pathetic and desperate about.

He gulps down iced-sugar tainted with a few drops of coffee. I like Glenn. He's never afraid to be honest, even if it's always brutal and heartbreaking. He knows that people don't choose their nationalities. He seems to like his job which is mostly to impart that the United States Citizenship and Immigration Services don't fuck around. They definitely do not. The amount of traps they lay for immigrants makes living here a minefield. Even getting one of the human beings on the phone who runs the immigration program is a feat.

Practically every time you want to speak to one of their reps, you usually have to clear out your day. Since they all work on east coast hours, I would usually have to get up around five in the morning here in LA, their eight in the morning, stay on hold for a few hours, get transferred up to the next level because the rep I'm speaking to isn't 'qualified'

"How much can I pay you to jerk me off underneath the tablecloth?"

I glance down to see his thing poking out from his tight jeans. It's rather large and grotesque. I wonder how long he's had it out. Nobody else seemed to notice. I guess that's why he had them set up the tablecloth like this. *Has he done this before?*

"Fifty thousand," I blurt.

"What?"

"I'll do it for fifty thousand."

He quickly puts it back in his pants as a waiter moves closer to fill our water glasses. When the waiter moves away, Neel shakes his head, flustered.

"That's way too much."

"Really? Seems pretty fair to me."

"Someone else did it for me for much less."

"How much did they do it for?"

"Four grand."

Fuck this asshole. I want to leave as soon as possible, but first I want to embarrass this pretentious prick. I put on a warm smile, "I'll do it for thirty thousand."

"Ten."

I grab my purse and begin to rise. He raises his hands in defeat, "Okay, thirty."

After I see the bank transfer pop up on my phone, I sigh. This is not how I expected my days in LA would be spent. Neel pops out his ugly thing and I grab it. He scoots forward so my hand is hidden underneath the tablecloth. I can feel it start to grow. He looks around the restaurant smugly. I start to pump and Neel's eyes roll back in bliss. I wave at a tired-looking, gangly waiter with a buzzcut with my free hand, making sure to keep silent so as not to alert Neel. The waiter approaches. As he gets closer, he sees my arm pumping and frowns.

I knock over Neel's half-empty margarita so it spills onto his lap, quickly extracting my hand. Neel screams as the cold alcoholic liquid hits his exposed protrusion and instinctively leaps up. The entire restaurant watches Neel flash his thingy. A woman a few tables over screams and a group of collared-shirted guys in a booth explode in laughter and pound the table with their fists. A large, muscly father orders his kids to look the other way, stands, lunges the short distance, and punches Neel smack dab in the forehead.

I wave to Neel from the sidewalk in front of the cantina. He's sitting groggily in the back of a cop car, which pulls away and off into the night. I feel a lot richer and very guilty for ruining so many people's afternoons. I wish I could say that was the grossest asshole I've ever met...

My name is Samantha. I've been living in Los Angeles for the last five years. I'm from Houston, Denver Harbor to be exact. It's not the most upscale part of the city, by a long shot. My dad's a middle school teacher and my mom works in hospital administration. They live in a tiny apartment and are most likely just scraping by. They don't discuss finances with me.

My mother is borderline obese, as are a lot of people in Houston. Thank god she works in a hospital, because she can get cheaper treatments for her 'condition' which is what she likes to call it. Really, she just gorges herself on food and never exercises. We don't get along. That's all I want to say on that.

I knew from a very early age that I wanted to get out of Houston, out of Texas, and out of the South, so after high school, I applied for a whole bunch of scholarships and loans for college and applied to practically every school on the West Coast. It worked because a year ago, I graduated from the University of Southern California!

LA is one of those giant cities in which you could spend your entire life and never see everything. You could probably spend ten lifetimes and not see everything. It's fun and wonderful. I absolutely could not see myself anywhere else.

USC was a whirlwind of drinking, drugs, boys, and stress. The first three probably caused the last to be so bad. I graduated with a major in Art and Design, which prepared me to make zero money, which blows cause I have at least six figures of student debt to pay off.

My passion is painting. I've known that I've wanted to be a painter since I was five and drew my family's dog Dude. The painting was so good for my age that my teacher tacked it up to the wall. Still, one of my proudest accomplishments.

Recently, my favorite things to paint are landscapes. There's something so calming about creating an entire perspective. You can add little details, literally whatever you want. In that small, 2D world, you are God!

Probably my favorite place in LA is the Getty museum. I especially like the Dutch painters, cause they paint such idyllic scenes. I wish I could paint that well.

I am able to live in a bougie apartment in Beverly Glen not through painting, duh, but through money I make online as an influencer and sugarbaby. I came into this semi-accidentally. In college, I made a public Instagram account to show off my paintings with the hopes to sell them. At first, I was posting a lot of photos of my work, but I only had less than a hundred followers, most of which were good samaritans from my private account.

One day, after failing an Italian quiz and getting ghosted by this dumb lacrosse player, I felt a little insecure and vulnerable, so I put on some blush and a push-up bra and posted a pic of me posing with an impression of a nectarine. After posting that, I got a few hundred followers in the first few hours. Lots of randoms commented, saying how much they liked the painting, how cute the fruit looked, and even got a few DMs asking for commissions.

I figured that people appreciated knowing the artist, so I started posing next to my paintings. In a few weeks, I had like five thousand followers. Some still wanted commissions but they all mostly turned out to be creeps. So many dick pics. Some guy offered me three hundred to send him a nude, so I blocked him.

Going through comments and DMs, I realized that my followers didn't actually care much about my paintings. I tried posting a pic of this really beautiful mountain landscape without myself in it, but maybe a quarter of people liked it, and it got no comments.

I decided to further test my theory by just posting a photo of me stretching in athleisure with the caption, "An active mind is a healthy mind" and it got more likes and comments than anything I've done before. A few dudes asked me if I had an OnlyFans, which I didn't at the time, of course.

Halfway through senior year, I had over three hundred thousand followers. I was promoting products through my posts and stories which were no longer about painting. It was strictly me in skimpy clothing doing fun things around the city. Small brands had DMed me to pose with their products. It was fun and easy. I thought of it as a side-gig, something to keep me afloat while I painted.

I became really popular at USC. Girls would come up to me on my way to class and ask me where I bought such and such, asking for selfies together, and inviting me to parties. Guys would come up and hit on me, often pretending that they didn't know I was insta-famous.

That dumb lacrosse boy suddenly wanted me back, but I started going to parties in Beverly Hills, Bel-Air, Laurel Canyon, and made influencer connects. USC parties seemed childish and boring. The parties I went to in the second half of senior year were like fancy, networking events with beautiful people and free drugs.

One girl, who I will not name because she has millions of followers, told me how easy it was to make loads of money on OnlyFans and Seeking Arrangements. She told me about this older movie producer who paid her tens of thousands of dollars at a time to simply have dinner with him. No sex, no kissing, no touching beyond a hug, was required. She told me I have the body and bust for it.

Then I graduated. No more dorms, no more meal plans, no more safety net. I was afloat on the open ocean with no sail or anchor. But at least I'm pretty. For a few months, I bummed around on friend's couches, often with guys but those stays always got messy. I tried applying to some service jobs, but I absolutely hated the rigid hours and low pay.

My mental health was deteriorating fast. I had to find a steady place to live, preferably alone. I was still making some money from influencing, but it barely paid for gas. I was reaching five hundred thousand followers and my posts were slowly but steadily turning more racy. I was almost doing it subconsciously, some internal drive to get more followers and therefore money.

I created an OnlyFans in the summer. I remember because I was staying at my friend Maddie's place and it was fucking hot in her apartment. I asked her to take some nudes of me, but she kept laughing because I really didn't know how to pose. She demonstrated each position, which helped but I remember thinking that nobody could find this much sweat sexy. I had sent like three nudes before that, all to a long term, now-ex boyfriend.

After making the pricing tiers and putting the link to it in my bio, the creeps came in like waves, growing after each post. After the first few months, spending several hours a day posting stories, responding to messages, and even recording some oddly specific videos, I was making a few thousand dollars per week.

Six months after graduation, I moved into my own place in a nice complex in Beverly Glen with a swimming pool and hot tub, which I've used religiously. I have enough space for my paintings, supplies, camera equipment, peloton, and even a nice sectional.

Another influencer messaged me about camming, which was another step I recently took. A few weeks ago, I made an account on Voypure.com, one of the top camming sites. Pretty much, I log on twice a day, spend a few hours talking to viewers with a remote controlled vibrator in my you-know-what. When viewers, mostly men, send me tips, the vibrator goes off. The bigger the tip, the longer and more intense the vibration. Sometimes I do private shows where I charge a single viewer by the minute.

I now advertise my OnlyFans and Voypure account on my Instagram, Twitter, and Tiktok. It's all connected and helps me gain a larger following. I'd bet I now have probably a few million followers collectively across all platforms. I also have a rotating cast of older sugardaddies who supplement my lifestyle with allowances, gifts, trips, and guilt-free sex.

And yes, I do show my face. When I originally made my art account, I didn't use my real name so I'm not that worried. The few people who followed my art account have been generally supportive of my change in direction. As of now, neither of my parents know anything about it and none of my relatives have said anything. My little fourteen-year-old cousin, Emily, might know something, but hopefully she doesn't do any further investigating. My parents must think I've been supporting myself through art shows and other part time jobs, but I don't care.

I'm saving money and having fun doing it. If I keep going, I'll be able to pay off my student loans in a year or two. Eventually, I will switch back to painting. It's my true calling and all this influencing and sex-work is just temporary. A means to an end.

I get up Saturday morning around eight. I like to get up

early, if you can call that early, usually to work out and then get brunch with some friends after.

I get on the Peloton and load up a scenic long distance ride in Southern Patagonia. I watch the funny looking llamas prance on the side for a minute before turning my attention to my phone. I've got a backlog of messages, comments, snapchats, and requests to respond to, but I take a short vid of me on my bike and post it to my Insta story. Then, I start the long slog of responding to everything.

Thirty minutes later, I'm done with my bike ride, but the notifications are coming in faster than I can deal with them, so I spend an hour on the couch on my phone. Finally, Laura, one of my best friends, facetimes:

"Oh my god, you won't believe what happened last night!" She starts off without any greetings.

"What happened? You were out in Santa Monica, right?"

"Yeah, at the Victorian, but then we went to Ryan's afterparty in Calabasas."

"Ryan Westin?"

"Uh huh. You remember a few weeks ago when that rapper guy DMed me? Lil Kaiser?"

"Of course," I lie.

"He was there but he was with that girl from that one show..."

"Which show?"

"The boring medieval one on HBO. Anyways, they're all snuggled up on the couch when we come in, but when he sees me, he perks up and she gets really annoyed. Ryan's all over me of course, which makes Lil Kaiser salty and he comes out on the patio looking for me..."

I listen to Laura's unremarkable story with feigned interest, peppering the conversation with affirmations and nods. After revealing that Lil Kaiser is a premature ejaculator, she informs me that brunch is off because the girls want to go out tonight and she wants to take a nap before.

I shrug, "Works for me."

Now that I think about it, I could use a fun night out. I know this is like the biggest first world problem ever, but it's, like, exhausting having to pretend to like guys for money. I haven't had a boyfriend in a few years and I'm starting to wonder if it's actually possible in my line of work. I've dabbled in dating apps, but the results are always disastrous. Every cute guy I come into contact with, who isn't delivering my food or walking down the street, is overtly paying me for my time. I enjoy it, but I would like to have somebody who I'm into for them.

CHAPTER 3

Night Out

The Bloody Orange is bustling. It's half past eight on Saturday night so people are starting to pour in for primetime hookah and drinks. The valet service is stretched thin and most tables have been reserved. Those who don't show up to their reservation within twenty minutes lose it.

Alvaro's section is the food-only section. No hookah allows for bigger tables and means that he's considerably more busy, but also making more tips. Already, there's been a drunken squabble between two adjacent tables over bumping chairs and Gordon, one of the bus boys, hasn't shown up yet. Alvaro's more stressed than usual. He spots a group of five beautiful girls crowding Maria's hostess stand. All the girls are looking up from their phones at the other patrons, hoping to see somebody cool enough to allow them to grace the restaurant with their presences. After a quick series of nods, the girls decide the other clientele is acceptable. Laura, a curly-haired, big-nosed girl, gives her name to Maria who leads them to a table in Alvaro's section.

Alvaro saunters into the kitchen, grabs a bottle of Jose Cuervo, and takes a swig. The dishwashers all yell, "Cabron!" in unison before going back to work. Alvaro grabs an order of appetizers and brings it out to a couple. He then glides over to the table of five girls.

"Good evening, Welcome to the Blood Orange, what can I get you started with?"

"I'll have a gin and tonic with no lime," Laura blurts like she's been waiting all night.

Matilda, a skinny blonde girl with blown-up lips orders, "A gold rush, please."

"This one," proclaims Kimberly, a red-headed girl with green eyes, pointing at the menu.

"The same," mumbles Caroline, an extremely thin, black girl with sharp cheekbones who hasn't cared to look at the menu. Alvaro makes another mark on the last order. He turns to the last girl and stifles a sharp intake of breath.

She's stunning. The first thing Alvaro notices is a constellation of dark freckles around an ever so slightly up-turned nose. He moves to her eyes, two orbs of brown, deep, earthy, and wise. She's fit. Her breasts are large. Alvaro can tell her butt draws looks from the way her hips bunch up around her waist as she sits. There's something calming and serene in her posture. Alvaro supposes she's half Asian, half Latina perhaps?

"Mojito, please."

Alvaro nods, writing this down. Her pronunciation of mojito sounds pretty gringa to him.

"Perfect, would you ladies like some food?"

They order one plate of pita bread collectively. Alvaro hopes they buy more drinks but doesn't let it show.

Forty five minutes later, all the girls are on their phones, sending out feelers for potential festive options. Samantha looks up from her phone at their waiter who moves gracefully toward their table to take a second round of drink orders. She studies him carefully.

He's tall but not gangly, probably six foot one. His straight dark hair hangs lazily over his forehead, framing a sharp jaw and two round, innocent eyes. He obviously works out and eats healthily, judging from the tight black uniform which conforms to a chiseled torso. He looks and sounds foreign, which is exciting. He gives off a creative vibe, like a tortured artist. Unfortunately, his job doesn't instill a sense of stability or wealth...

"Would you like any more drinks?" He asks the table, but comes to rest his gaze on Samantha before quickly averting it when he realizes that she's returning it.

"I think we're good, can we have the check?" Laura whines, glancing up from her phone with a sneer. Alvaro nods and moves off.

Samantha winces, tapping the table with her nails, "What're we doing tonight, guys?"

"Daisy invited us to her friend's house party in Silver Lake," offers Caroline.

"Sean says he can get us a table at Avalon," counters Matilda. Caroline boos and Matilda simply rolls her eyes. Laura winks at Samantha. Apparently, Sean and Matilda are a thing.

"I'm going to call an Uber to Daisy's friend's place," Laura states decisively, "I'm sorry, Matilda, but I have to let you know that Sean's brother Skyler tried to finger me at Nick's birthday."

"Really!? You're serious!?" screeches Matilda. Laura consoles her as Alvaro returns with the check. Samantha takes it from him, looks up and smiles.

Yes, he's poor, she thinks, *but he's cute. Shame.*

This guy has been nothing but nice and the one and half mojitos are making her feel adventurous. She places her debit card on the tray and he carries it away.

Alvaro looks down at the name on the card. *Samantha. What a beautiful name. If I wasn't working, I'd get her number. She's American as well. Maybe in another life...*

He brings back the card and the receipt, "Hope you all have a good night."

Alvaro wants to tell them, more specifically Samantha, to come back soon, but he thinks better of it. Best not to seem desperate and there's really no point.

The girls stumble through the restaurant, out onto turbulent Sunset Boulevard. Alvaro watches glumly as they pile into an UberXL and pull away. He sighs and looks down at the receipt. Samantha, the mythical princess, has left a twenty five percent tip. Alvaro picks up the paper and notices an extra line of scribbles underneath the signature line: nine beautiful, clearly written digits.

CHAPTER 4

Samantha

Even though my phone tells me the day of the week every morning, I don't really seem to register it that much anymore. My job isn't on a weekday schedule. I don't have set hours, which means extreme flexibility, but also I only get out what I put into it. There's no such thing as 'weekends'. Saturdays and Sundays are busier if anything.

My phone tells me it's Monday. Whatever. The weather is classic LA, relentlessly hot and smoggy. For lunch, I take a walk to the Grove wearing some pink short-shorts, a white tank top with frilly sleeves, and flip flops. My hair is done up in a ponytail. I have with me an old cloth Trader Joe bag in case I decide to pick up some produce at the farmer's market.

It's packed. Gross. Tourists waddle back and forth between empanadas, Brazilian steak, seafood, coffee, soft-serve, pizza, ostrich jerky, and French cuisine that would make a real frenchie gag. I buy a few ripe looking avocados and pomegranates.

I swim through the crowd towards the mall section of the Grove. Designer clothing stores loom up on either side and I have to restrain myself from getting sucked inside Lululemon. Barnes & Noble looms up on my right, three stories of books and puzzles. It always makes me feel guilty because I used to read a lot as a kid, but now I almost never do.

Up ahead is the movie theater. I stop and look up at the posters for the now-playing. Nothing looks good, in fact it all looks trash, except for a cartoon one with a dog and a cat.

A group of tall, hype-beast-looking guys whistle at me as they pass. I've learned to just ignore them. Fueling their fire can often come back to bite you. One time, a guy literally tried to bite me.

I feel my phone vibrate in my shorts, so I pull it out to find a message on Seeking Arrangements. *Gerald*, a particularly wrinkled old guy, wants to get dinner at Nobu in Malibu. I had sushi a few days ago, but it's hard to turn down Nobu, so I open the chat.

Gerald is offering not only to cover dinner but to give me $1000.

I respond, "*Hey baby. Could you cover my Uber there?*"

According to his profile, Gerald is in his seventies. Meh, I've been with older. I take a selfie in front of the fountains with my tongue sticking out and post it to my public snap story. Then I start the journey back.

As I'm crossing La Jolla, Gerald messages me back, "*Of course! What's your address? I'll send one at 6?*"

Yep, his age checks out. Early dinner and ignorance of online etiquette. A younger man would already know that I wouldn't give out my address first thing. I tap out a reply,

"Let's make it 7. Send the car to the Four Seasons on Doheny. Excited ;)"

Back in my apartment, I have a few hours to kill so I log onto Voypure. When I open up my cam, an email notification is automatically sent out to all my followers. In a matter of minutes, there are already two hundred viewers.

Usual cam sessions last from two to four hours, depending on how many tips are coming in. If there's more, I will stay on for longer. Often, when certain goals are reached, I have to fake an orgasm. It all depends. I have a 'tip menu' which details what I would do for different amounts. It's exhaustive, ranging from 'jump up and down' to 'oil with dildo'. If you want to know exactly what that means, guess you'll have to follow me.

I have three or four guys who are 'mods'. These are guys who I've never met before but they willingly help police my cam-room for nothing other than...well, I'm not exactly sure...they don't get paid. Maybe they get off on the small fantasy of being my 'protector' or something? Who knows.

People are extremely chatty today but not that focused. Two guys are arguing about some video game, so one of my mods kicks them out of the room.

As I answer some of stupid, predictive questions, I stand up and take time in adjusting my top. I'm wearing clothes, not much, but just enough so that the viewers have to pay me to take them off. The top adjustment gets the viewers excited and a few tips come through. One of the tips is large enough to buy 'flash tits' so I smile seductively and slowly peel my top down, making sure that I pause at the nipple and squeeze in just enough that my nipples pop out. I watch as my viewer count jumps up and more small tips flood in. The vibrator in me buzzes like crazy so I roll my eyes in theatrical pleasure. It's all about getting the viewers excited enough that they feel as if spending just a little bit more will get them there. It's not hard. You just have to learn how to reel them in and tease them.

After a bit, I'm cleaning oil off my butt from a tip that merited 'twerk with oil'. Even the cleaning gets some tips. A golden viewer requests a private C2C (Cam to Cam). The fact that he's golden indicates that he has more than a thousand dollars loaded into his account. He's requesting a private C2C which means that my cam will be hidden from all other viewers than him and I'll be able to see his camera. If I accept, he gets charged $10 a minute. I accept.

Of course, his camera is dark, meaning he's obscuring it somehow. About ninety percent of people who buy C2C start this way. I raise my eyebrow playfully and say, "Anybody home?"

A nervous clearance of the throat is followed by an uncovering of his camera. An extremely skinny southeast Asian guy sits in his gaming chair, stroking away on his small, erect thingy. A massive bottle of lotion sits next to his scrunched up face. He's not bad looking, a lot younger than I expected.

"Wooooow," I say, winking.

"Can you...can you..."

Either his English isn't the best or there's not enough blood in his brain. Eventually, he manages, "Could you please stick out?"

"Hm? Stick out?"

"Tongue. Stick out tongue...please."

I stick my tongue out and he finishes, deflating like an above ground pool getting punctured. Without saying anything else, he quickly shuts down the private C2C, most likely embarrassed and ashamed. Only a few times have guys finished and stayed after for conversation. I don't think they realize that I'd stay on as long as they are paying. One time, a girl from Belarus paid for a private just to practice her English. She was quite nice, but she did ask me to pretend to be her horny cousin...

Around six thirty, Gerald texts me the details of the Uber so I walk over to the Four Seasons which is just a block away. I've put on a tight black skirt and white blouse with a plunging neckline. My lacy black pushup bra forces my boobs tight against the blouse. My stilettos are white with tiny black ribbons above the toe. The Uber driver has trouble keeping his eyes on the road. He tries to make conversation with me, but I stay focused on my phone.

When I arrive at Nobu, I'm happy to find that Gerald looks like his pictures, so similar in fact that I'm almost suspicious he took the photos earlier in the day. Why does that make me suspicious? It's way better than having the pictures be, like, super outdated!

He's tall, or at least was at one point. He's got one of those slouched postures that a lot of older men get where their neck seems to lose strength and their shoulders and head roll forward. His suit's expensive and nicely ironed. I can tell he is not an experienced daddy.

"Nice to meet you," he says as we hug, "You're even prettier in person."

He smells like beer and mint. I hang my Gucci handbag on the back and sit down, making sure not to slouch.

"Nice to meet you too," I say with a formal smile. I try not to be too affectionate before a payment plan has been finalized.

"The ride over was okay?"

We small talk for a bit until the waiter comes over. She's a small brunette with very flat bangs and a mole above her left nostril. I think she's served me here before. From the way she glances at me, I can tell she knows what the dynamic is between Gerald and me. *It's pretty fucking obvious*, I want to say, *would I dress like this for my father?*

The waitress leaves and Gerald smiles and clasps his hand together like he's running out of things to say.

"Have you been here before?" he musters.

"No," I lie. I am not about to tell him, or anybody else for that matter, about the retired hockey player that used to snort lines of coke in the bathroom and try to feel me up under the table. Quickly glancing around, the hockey player is nowhere in sight. Phew. I do notice Julia Roberts sitting by the window.

"It's quite good," Gerald says, sipping his water, "The snapper with truffle is my favorite."

"So, what do you do for a living?"

"I'm the VP at..."

My mind begins to wander. How can it not? I study his wrinkles and nod as he talks, imagining what he would look like as a younger man. The first few times I went out with a man old enough to be my grandfather I didn't really know how to act. I've come to learn that older guys dating younger women want the girls to make them feel young but seasoned at the same time. We, the girls, have to act much older than we are, but remain helpless and ignorant. It's a fine line, but I've had plenty of practice.

"Interesting," I reply after he stops talking, "How did you get into that?"

On and on he goes. The waitress brings out the first few rolls. Even though I'm starving, I only take two cuts of each roll. Eventually, I mentally tune back in to hear him say, "Now I have to see her at Equinox with her **boyfriend**, that puffy asshole."

I dearly want to ask him to rewind but that would show I wasn't listening. Instead, I frown sympathetically. "Must be hard. I'm sorry."

"Yeah, well. I got the houses and the Porsche," he mumbles through a mouthful of blue crab. His eyes linger on my cleavage for a second, "I just installed a new hot tub. You should come over after dinner."

"I don't know," I respond sternly.

Gerald remembers who he's talking to and swallows, then burps but tries to cover it with his napkin. Gross.

"Of course," his eyes dart back down to my cleavage, "I was thinking two grand."

"To spend the night?"

"Only if you'd like."

"Excuse me," I stand, straightening out my skirt, "Be right back."

"Three grand?"

After grabbing my purse, I can feel the eyes of Gerald and the guy one table over on my back as I move through the tables towards the bathroom. Once inside the stall, I take out my phone and my wax pen, pressing the button several times to melt the wax a little before I send a plume into the fan above. Each hit brings down my pulse.

A few messages, some offers. Laura has sent me a snapchat video of her and some random guy at the Bungalow in Santa Monica. I respond with a black out photo and text, "*I might meet you out.*"

Seconds later, she replies in the chat, "*Come, bitch!*"

A few more puffs and some scrolls down Instagram. In the hallway right outside of the bathroom, there's a beautiful, huge painting of a beachside cabana on some unnamed Malibu grotto. I let a busboy by and stop to take in the work. Palm trees of various heights surround a quaint green two-story house with white trim and a brown deck. The beach below is golden brown and blue-gray water that sparkled in the light. The artist must have sprinkled on glitter right after painting. A blue surfboard sticks out of the sand, slightly off kilter. Two intricately done seagulls perch on the triangular roof, one preening itself and the other alert. A few other houses dot the greenish brown hillside above. There's not a single person shown which is smart because it would ruin the peace of it.

Something about it makes me shiver down my spine, not in a bad way. The simplicity of the house contrasted with the finely-done birds, foliage, and beach make it seem almost Manga-like, but it's not cheesy. Definitely not classy, though. I wonder what kind of stroke the artist used for the waves, because they did a great job of making it look choppy, but at the-

Buzz. Buzz. Gerald is texting me, "*You okay? They just brought out the black cod! How about $3500 for the night??*"

CHAPTER 5

Alvaro

I'm on my way to a shoot. It's an amateur short film directed by some guys I know somewhat through the Danielle Miller Studio. Antonio, good-looking, dumb guy, and Ravi, a quiet, skinny dude. Both are actors and Americans. They're young, probably both in their early twenties. I wouldn't be doing this if they hadn't promised to pay me $500 for the day.

Sunset going west is jammed, which is not uncommon for seven forty-five in the morning on a Tuesday. Some guy pulls aside me to the left, blaring house music so loud that his car shakes the road. I roll up my window and turn on the AC. I manage to just pass through the Doheny light as it turns red, so my car is the last car in the right lane. Some green hunk of junk pulls up to my right behind the row of parked cars to my right. It inches its front bumper towards mine, showing that it wants to cut off me.

Fuck this. I pull up ahead a little to show them that I'm not entertaining their stupid idea of getting one car ahead. If you entertain their tonterías, they'll think they're in the right. My display of dominance must piss the driver off because the green booger inches even closer in, now visibly in my lane.

!Chupa mi verga! I honk as I pull up even farther, almost rear-ending the car in front of me. The snot-mobile's window rolls down and a crack-infested woman with vomit colored hair and similarly colored teeth starts swearing at me, in some crude version of English.

The traffic ahead starts to clear and neither of us want to lose this battle. She actually forces her car into my lane and scrapes the side of my car with her side view mirror.

I roll down the passenger window, "Hey, fuck off, you piece of shit!"

"I'mma kill you!" She screams and throws something small and hard at my door. I think it was a battery. For several seconds, we're driving side by side in one lane. I see a few pedestrians filming. I don't need this shit. What am I doing?

I hit the brake. She pulls ahead, flinging a middle finger out her window, and honking a few times victoriously.

At the next light, she's in front of me. I shake my head, feeling cowardice and rage battling it out in my churning stomach. Then, without warning, her door flies open and the beast is on the move towards me. She's brandishing a 7-Eleven smoothie with her surprisingly toned, spider-like arms. The sight of a human walking in the road paralyzes me.

"Shit," I regain mobility and furiously paw at my windows, closing them just before an explosion of blue ice covers my windshield and side window. Her hand slaps the windshield three times in rapid succession, jiggling the oozing blue coat. I turn on the wipers. Cars are honking all around us.

"Bitch ass motherfucker!" screeches the banshee. She heads back to her car, but doesn't get in. It looks like she's fishing around her front seat for another projectile, but lucky for me, the traffic is beginning to clear around us, so I quickly nab a space in the left lane and zoom ahead.

A few blocks and windshield-wipes later, everything but my heart rate is back to normal. I check the rearview a few times, but the slushie-demon and her vomit ride are nowhere to be seen.

I pull my car through the open gates of some crazy big property in Holmby Hills. Holmby is the rich part of Beverly Hills. Yeah, you're reading that correctly. There's a skeleton of a mansion surrounded by well-trimmed grass surrounded by tall hedges. Ravi told me it's his boss' fixer-upper and that they can use the site to shoot a horror short during one of the days there's no construction. It definitely looks like an interesting set, very creepy.

There is already a line of cars parked crookedly down the driveway. The crew must have arrived here early.

Nobody is anywhere to be seen, but I assume they are inside, so I stroll up to the front door which is halfway painted dark green - almost the same color as the crazy rage-filled bitch that attacked me fifteen minutes ago. I shiver.

The inside of the house is less finished than the outside, plastic sheets line the floors, open drywalls look like they are about to crumble, and wires dangle from the ceiling. A few c-stands lie flat in the corner. Out of the ceiling-high doorway walks a short Asian girl, wearing a french hat. She smiles nervously when she sees me, "You must be Alvaro! I'm Billy, nice to meet you."

"Sorry I'm late."

"All good, we're still setting up. You have updated sides, right?"

I wave my phone around, "I have what was sent to me last night."

Billy frowns, thumbing through her phone, "Ah, actually, Antonio just sent out some revisions. Looks like he forgot to CC you. There ya go!"

My phone dings with the email of freshly updated sides. Wonderful. The director forgot to send one of the lead actors updated sides. This gives me hope.

"How much has changed?"

"Not much, just the first and fifth scene, the party ones," Billy says, leading me farther into the interior of the house, "Oh, and some small tweaks during the pool scene."

Before I can complain, we arrive in what will most likely be a kitchen, where the entire cast and crew stand around a large, white marble island. Cabinets without doors line the walls. Antonio and Ravi hug me and introduce me to the rest.

Everybody is younger than me and, with the exception of Billy and the two lead actresses, male. Ten people in total, including me. Michelle, a French guy with a thick head of spiky blonde hair and even thicker accent, talks to me like we know each other already from Danielle Miller Studio, but I can't remember him for the life of me. He's the cameraman. Carley, one of the lead actresses, nods her dainty shaved head at me, then returns to her hypnotic fixation on Antonio. Phil, a large, ugly American guy who communicates in grunts and twitches, is Sound. His headphones seem permanently attached to his greasy head.

Halley, the other actress, is a blonde, midwesterner who looks like she went through recent plastic surgery on her nose, the skin around it lotioned to oblivion. Charlie and Gordan work lights, two scruffy gringos who I have trouble separating since they both said their names simultaneously and they look like the yin and yang of the average Melrose thrift store shopper.

An hour later, we're still in the kitchen, listening to Michelle and Antonio argue about how to properly white balance the camera. It's Antonio's camera, but Michelle claims to know how to use it better. Billy is googling furiously on her phone and Phil is watching football on his. Charlie and Gordan are smoking cigarettes. Everybody else, including me, waits impatiently.

"I'm going to go practice my lines in the backyard," I say and exit with no acknowledgement that anybody heard me.

"*What the fuck are you doing here, bro?*" I recite to the broken fountain in the back. Ah, yes, original, expertly crafted dialogue. Sorkin would be proud. This whole project is starting to seem worth $500 less by the minute. Antonio and Michelle are still arguing about white balancing and it's already almost lunch.

Halley comes out and walks over to me, "Wanna run lines?"

"Sure," I scroll to our scene, "Can I ask you something?"

"What?" She pulls out her phone.

"How do you know these guys?"

"Antonio and Ravi? I don't really. They reached out to me through Backstage."

For those who aren't familiar with the trials of the struggling Los Angeles actors, Backstage is a website for smaller productions and actors to connect. Anybody trying to get content for their reel or casting their short film will most likely use it. Like anything digital with desperate people, you're bound to run into some weirdos. Halley hasn't done anything weird yet, but I'm ready for whatever comes.

"I know 'em through school. They were just as organized as they are now."

Halley nods, sitting on the fountain ledge, "I've been a part of more disastrous projects."

"Do tell," I click my phone closed and sit next to her.

"Well," Halley also puts her phone down, "I think the worst one was when there was a scene with flaming shots. It was some stupid comedy about alcoholics. The director wasn't a total idiot, but she was really trying to rush. One of the actors didn't blow out the flame enough before taking the shot and poured the flame onto his face. He burned for a good ten seconds as he was running around."

"Oh my god!"

"Yeah, luckily there was a pool nearby which he jumped in. Still got really bad burns on half his face. He came from a family of lawyers so it got messy, but it ended his career. He left Los Angeles the next month."

"Did you know him very well?"

Halley shrugs wistfully, "Kind of. We had done a few things together. But you know what they say. Once you leave LA, you never come back."

Is that true? I think back on all the people I've known who have moved away from Los Angeles. Have any of them ever come back? Sure, they've visited but I can't think of anybody who's moved back. Jackson did, but he lives with his family in Santa Clarita, which is not really Los Angeles...

Daintily pinching the bridge of her nose, Halley clenches her eyes shut in seemingly deep concentration, "I can't find Derrick anywhere! We should call the police!"

"Excuse me?" I say, wondering what the hell she's talking about. Is this her weirdness coming out finally?

"My first line?" Halley looks at me like I'm slow.

"Ah, okay...um...oh yeah," I scrunch up my face in fear, "I don't have any reception! We're fucked!"

Before we can go on, the rest of the crew spills out into the backyard. Michelle grumbles at Halley and me, "You two good to go?"

"Rehearsed and ready," Halley proclaims, giving me a sly wink.

It's almost midnight. Unsurprisingly, the filming was a disaster. Pretty much every scene ended with Antonio or Ravi saying, "We'll fix it in post." Hopefully it will never see the light of day. At least I got paid. And Halley's number!

Even though it's longer and more windy, I've decided to take Mulholland for the ride back. Sunset would be much faster but I want to go to my favorite view point, a few minutes off of Mulholland into Laurel Canyon. Not many people know about this, which makes it the best in my book. The signs around say no parking, but a tow truck would take forever to get there. I'm not going to tell you how to get there.

Once parked, I walk down a little dirt path that takes me to a little plateau overlooking all of West Los Angeles. I can see sparkling lights all the way down to the dark, forbidden hills of Palos Verdes. A spotlight flicks back and forth somewhere Downtown. That's gotta be a hazard for pilots, no? The faint sounds of sirens and honking are suddenly drowned by music from a party in a house just below the look out in Trousdale Estates.

Once you leave LA, you never come back.

Halley's words are haunting me. If I don't find somebody to marry soon, I'm screwed. Eventually, I'll have to go back to Mexico and when I do, I won't be able to come back for a long time, unless I get the Green Card. If I don't get a Green Card, my chances of making it as an actor are nothing.

A chilly gust pushes up the canyon, making me shiver. I throw on a sweatshirt from my car and put my hands in its pocket. There's some crumpled-up piece of paper. I pull it out and unravel it. It's an old receipt.

The receipt with that girl's number! She gave me **her** number. She wants me to text her. Worst case scenario, she doesn't respond. Best case scenario, we fall in love, get married, I can become a citizen, we have lots of kids, and I ascend into Hollywood stardom. Fuck it.

CHAPTER 6

Samantha

Who's Alvaro? He's got a LA area code, but how he got my personal number is beyond me. I never give out my actual phone number unless there's been a heavy payment. Maybe it's some college guy from several phones ago? Or maybe one of my daddies gave out my number?

All he texted was, "*Hey, Samantha, it's me Alvaro, from a few weeks ago. Wanted to see if you'd like to get dinner sometime?*" Come on dude, be a little more specific if you don't want to get blocked.

I put my phone down to try and enjoy sitting in the hot tub. I'm exhausted. It was a full day of hot yoga, rough sex with a very aggressive studio head, and a taxing marathon call/fight with my mom.

I feel like I should block this number, but I can't stop wondering how Alvaro got my number. Time for some recon.

"*Sorry, I got a new phone. Who is this?*"

I click send and wait. No text bubbles. I place my phone on the edge of the hot tub and close my eyes.

A fleck of red, like dark blood. A spattering of orange, cross hatching with the red. Blue wavy lines that turn emerald green swim over and under the warm summer mix. Then, an amorphous figure, small and seemingly in the dis-

Brrrrh. Brrrrh. A notification yanks me out, with a bit of whiplash. I dry my hands off on a nearby towel to check. Alvaro has responded, "*From the Bloody Orange. You left me your number on the receipt...*"

Oh yeah! The cute waiter. I totally forgot about him. I pick up my phone and am about to tap out a reply when my phone slips from my hand and plops into the seething hot tub water, sinking quickly to the bottom. I stare at it, making no move to retrieve it. There's no point. But there's a weird feeling surging through me, something I haven't felt in years. It's butterflies, actual flutters in my stomach. It's like I want to text this guy back just to talk with him.

At the Apple Store, Ron sets up my new phone. He's a scruffy Armenian guy who always goes out of his way for me. He's never creepy, thank god, just extremely bubbly and helpful.

"You backed up your iCloud, right?" He says in his thick accent while peering through reading glasses at the shiny, new iPhone.

"Yep."

"Just log into your iCloud and we should be good to go," Ron hands me the phone, "What was it this time?"

"A boy," I grin meekly.

Ron shakes his head, chuckling.

The date is on the books. I'm going to meet him at the Tocaya in Westwood. Not the most upscale place, his idea, but I'm actually incredibly excited. I got Matilda to come over and help me get ready. She won't stop gushing about how uncharacteristic tonight will be for me.

"A real date with a guy! A real guy!"

Finally, I tell her that I'm leaving, even though I don't plan on calling my Uber for another hour. I can't stand her saying, "Oh my god, you're really going to do this!?" one more time.

My makeup is quite subtle, really only some concealer and mascara. I've been blessed with naturally clear skin, so acne is rare. I wonder if Alvaro is the kind of guy who likes lots of makeup or none at all. I bet most guys wouldn't even notice. I should show up tonight with minimal makeup and go to the next date with it caked on to see if he says anything. I'm getting ahead of myself. Let's get through tonight.

When I'm five minutes out, I begin to have second thoughts. I don't even know this guy. He's some stranger. I have no online verification of who he is, where he's from. He could be a serial killer or a scientologist or a Trumper!

Chill. We're meeting in a public place and I'll be able to discern how I feel about him safely. Matilda knows where I'm going and is tracking me. I can always leave whenever I want.

Once I get out of the Uber, I hit my wax pen a few times which helps my nerves. Through the window, I see him, sitting in a booth in the back, looking at a menu. He's still as cute as he was a few weeks ago. He pushes his floppy black hair out of his face and clenches his sharp jaw with indecision. I shove my wax pen in my purse and enter.

CHAPTER 7

Alvaro

!Que guápa! This girl is vastly out of my league. It's hard to believe that she gave me her number and even harder to believe that she's walking towards me with her freckles. She actually came!

"Welcome," I say dumbly, instantly regretting it. Why the fuck would I say welcome?

She laughs as she comes near, "Do you work here too?"

"No, I'm just incredibly nervous." Shut up! Shut up!

"Well, you should be," she says, gliding towards me for a hug. Her breasts squish into my side and her heavenly scent assails me. I feel dazed. Once we're seated it's hard to look anywhere but at her dark freckles.

She's wearing some makeup, but not that much, which I like. She definitely cares about her appearance but isn't obsessed with it. She doesn't look plastic, which some guys are definitely into. Not me.

"I have to be honest, I'm shocked you gave me your number," I find myself saying.

"Why?" She crinkles her nose so that the freckles hop up and down.

"Well, you're...you know..."

"...What?"

I feel my face grow warm, "Can't imagine you're giving out your number left and right."

She raises a perfect eyebrow smugly, "You'd be surprised."

"Well anyways. I'm glad you replied."

"Where are you from?"

"Mexico. I've spent way too much money on accent reduction classes, so that's a big bummer to hear."

"No, I mean, your English is great, but there's a slight hint. I'm sure you use it to your advantage. Why would you want to get rid of an accent?"

"It's beneficial for my career to get rid of it."

"Actor?"

She guessed it quickly. This could be dangerous. I gotta tread carefully. One wrong move here could jeopardize everything. I quickly run through some options and decide to play it safe, "Maybe, one day."

"Wouldn't a latin accent help you with your career?"

"If I wanted to be type casted! What about you?"

Samantha stares back at me. She doesn't speak for nearly five seconds, then shrugs. She looks down at the menu. What was that? Is she a drug dealer or something? Why is she pausing for so long? Does she come from money?

"I paint," she glances up, "But I pay the rent by being an influencer."

"Oh man, so you're a social media star?"

"Yuck," she points to the register hurriedly, "We order up there, right?"

Later, we're in the booth together picking at chip crumbs. She's laughing at my list of hypothetical band names. We've reached the point of the conversation where it feels smoothly scripted, even though there are no sides. Witty references come easily and pauses punctuate them perfectly. I wish improv was always this easy.

"Coptic Pope would be a lot better than Alvaro and the Brown Loogies."

"Yeah, but definitely more...polemico."

"Polemico?"

"Umm, like starts a lot of arguments?"

"Controversial?"

"See, my English is not entirely perfect."

"Polemico could be an English word for all I know."

"Fair enough."

I have no clue what time it is. I tap my phone. We've been sitting here talking for almost an hour and half. She crosses her arms playfully, "Somewhere to be?"

"No, not at all," I venture, "This has been really fun."

She tips an ice cube from her water cup into her mouth, and crushes it immediately, "Aren't you glad I gave you my number?"

The workers behind the counter are starting to give us mad looks, so I suggest we walk down to a bar up the street that we find on Google maps. We find a divey college bar full of preppy UCLA kids.

I notice that Samantha is carefully scanning the place like

she's trying to find where a bomb is hidden. She's got her hands up around her chest.

"This okay?" I ask. She just shrugs back but doesn't walk any farther into the bar. Her gaze rests on a booth in the back where a group of large football players have spotted her and are exchanging hushed, excited conversation.

Do they know her? Does she know them?

"Actually, I'm pretty tired," Samantha suddenly proclaims, turning towards me and smiling sweetly, "I really did have a good time, though."

"Can I give you a ride home?"

"Hmmm, I don't know…"

I would feel bad about making her take an Uber home, especially when I have my car, but at the same time, I don't want to make her feel creeped. How much do I press until it becomes rude or weird? I'll just let her decide.

"Whatever you'd like."

"Okay, you can give me a ride home, but that's it. Seriously. No asking to come in an 'see my place.'"

I give her a classic American salute, "Ma'am, yes, ma'am!"

She laughs, a series of high-pitched squeaks each ending in a snort. I think I'm in love.

CHAPTER 8

Samantha

"So what happened?"

Laura sits across from me in the lobby of the West Hollywood Equinox. We're sitting in some plush, green chairs. She's wide-eyed, completely focused, and not glancing at her phone, so she must really want to hear about my date with Alvaro.

"It was really fun. We went to eat and talked for a while."

"That's it!?"

"Well, we tried to go to this bar after, but I bailed because I think some guys, like, recognized me. I didn't need Alvaro to see that."

Laura nods and scratches her neck. She's always been jealous of my fame, clout, online presence, whatever you want to call it. She's tried to cultivate the same following but it's never turned out as well. I hate to say it, but she just doesn't have the look. She works the front desk at Lionsgate, which I keep telling her is a great foot-in-the-door to a lot of cool entertainment jobs, but she doesn't seem to actually like take this to heart and pursue it. Last time I checked, I think she's hovering around ten thousand followers. I passed ten thousand followers in college.

I go on, "He hasn't texted me yet. It's only been a day, though."

"No goodnight text?"

"Nothing."

She's definitely secretly pleased by this. She purses her lips, "You tell'em what you do?"

"Kind of. I told him I was an influencer."

I don't mention that I barely slept last night thinking about how to break the rest of what I do to him. If I want things to continue, and **I do**, then eventually, it'll all have to come out.

Erewhon is packed. It's disgusting. Normally, they are usually pretty empty right before closing, but there must be some event going on at the Grove, because I'm having to squeeze my cart through oblivious shoppers. Laura decided to go home.

My phone is buzzing, but I just want to get out of this fucking grocery traffic before I answer it. There's too many bodies in here. I'll just go to Bristol Farms.

Once I'm finally out and standing down the block from the store, I look at my phone. Some random number called me with a 463 area code. A quick search tells me Indianapolis.

I'm not going to call it back. I don't know anybody from Indianapolis. Cars race down the street that separates the Grove and I from Pan Pacific park, a small dirty stretch of dead grass, unleashed dogs, and homeless. If it's important, they'll call again.

As if reading my mind, the number starts calling me. This time, I pick up.

"Hello?"

Some muffled fumbling then a clearing of the throat, then a man blurts, "Hi, is this Samantha?"

"Who is this?"

"This is, um, Scott Hillcrest from United Models. I came across your instagram page recently and I'm very interested in representing you. Would you be willing to be flown out to New York?"

"United Models?"

"Yes, ma'am."

"How did you get my number?"

"Sorry, what?"

"How...did you...get...my number?"

"Well, we have a directory, you know, of potential...clients, and..."

"Fuck off, creep."

I hang up and block the asshole. This is not the first time some jerk off has gotten my personal and called under the guise of something or other. I fell for it the first couple of times, but luckily I stopped them before anything got out of hand. This was different. This guy knew my real first name. Somebody must have leaked it along with my number. Several of my high paying clients have my number and know my name, so it could be them. Why would they give it out like that? Were they paid?

And I know what you're thinking. Samantha, you're crazy!

What if that was an actual modeling job? You just ruined your chances at reaching the upper echelons of the fashion world! I can tell you now, that that wasn't a real modeling agency. An authentic one wouldn't reach out over the phone like that, with that lack of confidence, and wouldn't do it from an Indianapolis area code. A real agency would reach out over email first to set up a call or a meeting. That was a creepy guy who couldn't think of a better way to keep me on the phone.

The only other person, besides close friends, family, and daddies, who has my name and number is Alvaro. He wouldn't give out my info like that, would he? Why would he? I barely know the guy, but he seemed so nice! God, I fucking despise men.

Right on cue, a crusty, older man with a horrible comb over pulls his Mercedes, rolls the passenger window down, and starts beckoning me over with two fingers, the creepiest way possible. I escape into the depth of the Grove where, thankfully, no one can drive.

Later, I sit in my apartment and stare at a blank canvas. I've laid out all the colors on my palette, selected the right brushes, and even did a little flipping through a collection of H. Bosch landscapes. Still, nothing comes to mind. I can't think of a single thing.

My phone buzzes, it's from this guy named Derrick in New Jersey on Seeking Arrangements. He's probably asking for some feet pics as he's done in the past. I quickly open it and yes, he's offering three hundred for a few angles. I snap away, making sure to point my toes straight. I tell him okay.

His Venmo hits my account so I send off the photos. He also sends a few dick pics which I delete immediately.

I put my phone on Do Not Disturb and turn once again to the blank canvas. Closing my eyes, I try to reimagine the red, orange, and blue mixture I had started to see the other day, but all I can picture is Alvaro. His slightly crooked smile across the booth.

A call bursts through my reverie. Dammnit, I thought I had this thing on silent? It's my dad, whose contact is a favorite which means his call will go through Do Not Disturb.

"Hey, Dad."

"Hi, Sweetie. Sorry for the late call, I just opened a kind of worrying letter."

I blink rapidly, thanking the lord that this is not a video call. Wouldn't want him to see how red my eyes are.

"What is it?"

"Another letter from that collection agency. They're asking about your student loans."

"Oh, yeah, could you send it to me?"

"Sure, I'll do it first thing in the morning."

"No, Dad, just take a picture of it and send it to me."

"Oh, okay," he says before murmuring something away from the phone. Mom's probably trying to tell him something in the background. "Honey, are you still there?"

"Yes."

"It's a lot of money. You know we're trying our best to help, just Mom's treatments just got extended and they're raising the rent here..."

I can tell Dad'll keep going until I verbally acknowledge their inability to help pay.

"It's okay, Dad, really. I got it. You don't need to worry."

"Well, Sammy, I'm a little worried. Mostly, I feel bad. I...we want to help you."

"It's fine, I'm working hard here, I'll be able to pay off everything."

Dad's voice brightens, "How is work going by the way? Any new shows coming up?"

"Probably in a few months," I use my standard vague response, knowing full well that my parents are too stingy to actually come out and visit me. "Things are going well. I met somebody."

"A boy!?"

"Yes, Dad, a boy. I'm straight, despite what Mom says."

I hear Mom grumble in the background. Dad sighs, "Sam, you know we would love you no matter who you end up with. Unless they're a Democrat!"

My father cackles, pleased with himself. I can't help but snort with him, relieved to hear he still has dad-jokes on tap. A rush of loneliness suddenly makes me want to buy a plane ticket and go home, at least for just a weekend, but it quickly fades when I remember my mother would be there.

"I love you, Dad."

"Love you too, sweetie. I've gotta run, but I do want to learn more about this boy. He's not a Democrat, is he?"

"Bye, Dad."

CHAPTER 9

Samantha

To me, second dates are more nerve wracking than first dates. First dates are an intro, dipping your toes into the water. Yes, you know that if there **is** a second date, you've established there's a strong mutual attraction and conversation comes easily enough, but the second date is where you tend to dive deeper into the psyche of the other person. You feel slightly more comfortable with them so you tread farther out into unknown waters to see if you can still float. Not all of my relationship metaphors are water themed, I swear.

Or this could just be me. I don't know, I guess I haven't gone on that many actual dates, let alone second dates. In college, hook-up culture was all I knew. High school, I had two long-term boyfriends. I'm really only trying to explain why I'm, like, so freaking nervous right now!

Alvaro suggested that we go to a movie for our second date, with drinks after. I agreed before I knew what the movie was. He wants to go see a horror called Tiller's Cross or Stiller's Den or something like that. I **hate** horror movies, but I'm not about to counter his idea with the newest Pixar movie. I don't want him thinking I've got the cinematic tastes of a child, even though, I guess technically I do...

I'm waiting for him in the food court of the Century City Mall food court. It's in the evening so most of the other shoppers are families, business people meeting for afterwork drinks, and unruly mallrats clinging to the mall's disgusting public furniture.

Standing near the entrance to the theater, I adjust my blouse, making sure to smooth out any creases. I'm freaking out because there's a stain on the knee of my capris, but I'm hoping Alvaro won't notice. He sure looks casually dapper, strolling towards me in jeans and a collared shirt. Thank god we dressed to the same level.

"Hey," he says warmly as we hug, cupping my back gently, "How's it going?"

"I'm good. How are you?"

"Pretty good. Excited to see this movie."

"Me too!" Not.

"You a big Danielson fan?"

"Uh, not really. What else has he done?"

He rattles off a list of movies that sound like the names of bars in Silver Lake that have gone out of business. I shake my head.

He smirks, "Not a big horror fan, I take it?"

"Sorry."

"We can watch something else!"

"No, no!" I wave my sweaty hands, "I'm down to try it."

"Are you sure? Really, not a big deal. There's a sci-fi out directed by Mick Darmony, got a ninety-six on rotten tomatoes?"

My facial expression sets him off laughing and he places a hand on my shoulder tenderly, "Come on."

Once inside the lobby, we look at current movie posters. The only one that looks remotely enticing is the kids movie about a cat and a dog that have to go on an adventure to rescue their young owner. We know this is what it's about because after I point to its poster, he pulls up the trailer on his phone for us to watch. He agrees with the tiniest hint of disappointment.

"Are you sure?" I plead, "I don't want you to pay double for tickets."

He smiles, sliding his phone back into his pocket, and waves reassuringly, "Not a problem."

I can tell that he's bummed, so I peck his cheek, surprising myself as well. He blinks and grins. There's a bit of my red lipstick on his face. For a split second, I almost move to wipe it off, but think better and leave it. Touching his cheek would be waaay too intimate.

"Holy shit!" Alvaro cries as we bounce out of the theater, an hour and half later, "That was incredible!"

"I know! The scene where they find the broken collars? And the dancing scene!"

"En serio," he murmurs as we stand in the middle of the hallway, letting people flow around us, "Not going to lie, I was not looking forward to that, but that was...it was one of the funniest movies I've seen in a while."

"Kids' movies are the best. It's pretty much all I watch." My hands are dry enough to playfully slap his shoulder.

"Still wanna get a drink?"

We're in Rodrigo's, a cocktail bar in the mall, at a table all the way in the back. The decor is trying hard to be Spanish with a medieval twist which doesn't really go well with the all-Mexican menu. I've ordered a ceviche and Alvaro has some enchiladas with black mole.

"Is it rude to ask how this compares to real Mexican food?" I tease.

He shrugs, popping a piece into his mouth, "Not bad, actually. If I see mole negro, I'm gonna order it. My mom always used to make it, so it's tradition."

I'm jealous that he's close with his mom. He hasn't mentioned his dad, but I don't want to pry too deep too quickly. Also, the way he says 'mole negro' makes me want to drag him into the handicap stall and touch his cheek. Shut up.

"I'm the same way with pesto pasta. My uncle used to make one with dried tomatoes. I have dreams about it, ugh."

"He lives in Texas as well?"

"Boston. We visited him a lot when I was young. Love to go visit when work calms down."

Alvaro wipes his face with his napkin and raises an eyebrow, "I didn't know influencing was so intense. Tell me more. Do you like it?"

Oops.

"It's okay. It's flexible." Now, you're contradicting yourself. "I mean, it depends. I have a lot of...events I need to attend here, but it's not, like, a nine to five kind of thing, obviously."

"How many followers do you have on Instagram? I'll be honest, I tried to stalk you, but couldn't find your account."

Here's the conundrum. If I tell him the real number, he's gonna want to see my profile. When he sees my page, he's going to discover my OnlyFans link. Then he'll know and probably find out about the sugarbabying. But if I don't tell him, I'll be lying. Not a great start to any relationship. Also, should I confront him about my number getting out? No, it's definitely not him, the weirdo caller knew about my Instagram page and Alvaro doesn't. Or does he and he's just trying to seem above it? If Alvaro gave my number away to somebody who knew my socials, he'd know my Instagram, which of course would show my OnlyFans, and he hasn't been acting weird or anything tonight. Maybe he's already seen the OnlyFans link on my Instagram and it doesn't bother him. But that would mean that he could have been the one to sell my personal number and name. Is he lying to me? I gotta show him, cause if I want this to go on, he'll find out eventually and it's the only way to gauge whether or not he's the one who sold my personal and name. And if he's lying and selling my info, do I want this to go on? Am I thinking about this too much? Or not enough?

"Around eight hundred."

"That's it? I have like nine hundred!"

"Thousand. Eight hundred thousand."

Alvaro stares at me like the live action version of Billy when his pet dog and cat rescued him at the end of the movie we just saw. I watch in slow motion as he pulls out his phone, flicks open his Instagram, and holds it up to me expectantly. Okay, so he's either a really good actor or he's genuinely never seen my Instagram.

"It's embarrassing."

"Come oooooon!" His eyes roll up and he shakes his phone at me.

I grab it and pull up my profile. He takes it back, inspecting it carefully. He glances back at me with a sly smile. I'm wondering if he can see my heart pounding through my shirt and the perspiration glomming onto my palms.

"You have an OnlyFans?"

"Just to make some extra cash!" I half-scream.

"What else would it be for?" he chuckles, which makes me feel a little better. He scrolls and taps for a bit. I pretend to find the grain of the table extremely engaging.

"Nothing too racy. It's so stupid."

"Wow," he murmurs, his fingers stopping, "Wow."

"What?" I lean over hastily. He turns the phone to show a photo of me at the beach in downward dog. I can feel my face boiling so I cover it with my sopping hands. "Oh god!"

"So, I'm on a date with a famous model?"

"Not famous. It's just a way to make money, to pay the rent. It's really stupid, I've been thinking about taking it down, you know, I just got into it and it's hard to turn the money down. It's...It's..."

"Hey!" he cuts me off, locking his phone and putting it away, "It's all good! I don't care!"

"Really?"

"Yeah! I think it's cool. If you're able to do it, why not?"

"Even the OnlyFans part?"

"Hell yeah. All the more power for you. As long as you're safe?"

"Yes. Thank you. Still, not my passion, not my end goal."

Alvaro cocks his head inquisitively, "Which is painting?"

"Yeah."

"Why don't you advertise your paintings on your accounts?"

"That's how it got started. I still have some, it's just way on the bottom of the page. I guess people were more interested in my body than my art."

"People are idiots."

"You've never even seen my art? Could be terrible for all you know."

"Show me some!"

Is he serious? Is he just asking this so he can get into my pants? If so, am I going to let him into my pants? What do I show him? AAAHHH!

I shake my head, "It'd be doing them an injustice to show you on a tiny screen."

He takes another bite of enchilada, getting some mole on his chin. That didn't go badly. He wasn't lying which means he's not the person who sold my info. I point playfully to my chin and he wipes his clean. Then I point to my cheek, and he wipes it clean again even though it was already clear.

"And here," I say, pointing this time to my forehead. He rolls his eyes. Too cute.

"Well, I guess you'll have to show me some of your work in person."

"Are you trying to get an invitation over? So early, nice try."

"You figured me out."

When we arrive back at my apartment, all I can think about is how messy Alvaro must think it is. I swing the door open and sigh, "Come in. Shoes off."

"Woah, nice!" Alvaro looks around with his mouth hanging down, "This place is so clean! Do you have roommates?"

Okay, that's good he doesn't think the place is gross, but what does that say about his standard of cleanliness? He's definitely asking about roommates to see if it's okay to hook up.

"Nope, just me!" I set my purse down on my dining room table and face Alvaro, who stands in the door inspecting every inch of the apartment. He seems to be in awe.

"You live here alone?" He echoes in disbelief, "You can afford that off the money you make as an influencer?"

I nod, unsure. Ah, that's why he was asking.

"I'm sorry, I didn't mean it like that, like I'm surprised that you can afford this, I just don't know how much somebody makes with that stuff. I am kind of impressed. If you don't mind me asking, how much do you pay for rent?"

"$2100."

It's actually $2600. My lie still seems to floor him. He slips off his shoes, walks over to the couch, and sits down gently as if the couch might fall apart at any moment. I feel like a wild animal has been let loose in my apartment.

He looks back at me with that same nervous, slack jawed expression, "So, are you going to show me your work?"

"Oh," I'm a little stunned, totally having forgotten that's why he came over. I head into my bedroom, grab a few finished canvases, and bring them out to him. I stand in front of him, holding them so they face away from him, "So these are really just first drafts, ideas for bigger projects."

"Okay," Alvaro perks up anticipatorily.

Suddenly, my knees start to wobble and I can feel sweat start to build up in my palms, a horrible response to anxiety I've had since I was a kid. Where is my wax pen? That's a horrible response I picked up in college.

"Uh, never mind. These are not the ones I want to show you," I quickly move to my room, shielding the paintings from him. Alvaro throws his hands up and laughs.

I return with a notebook of sketches. I often bring this little book around to sketch in places that I have to wait. Somehow I feel more confident sharing this as there's less color. Less to judge me on. The sketches are more casual, something which I'm not putting in as much effort as paintings.

Alvaro takes the notebook and starts to flip through it. I watch him, looking for any indication of disgust or confusion. All I see is delight. I think I'm in love.

CHAPTER 10

Samalvaro

Alvaro and Samantha sit on the couch for two hours. Flipping through her sketchbook, he starts to become comfortable enough to ask her questions. "What inspired you to do this? Why are there so many geese? Have you ever considered trying a graphic novel?"

She's enthralled by his enthrallment. It's been many, many years since someone other than her father has genuinely complimented her on her work. She hasn't really put much of it out there, but it's still nice to know she's still got it. He actually likes what he sees and feels as if he's getting a peek into a real part of her.

The sketchbook brings up conversations of the past. Samantha divulges her rocky childhood and how her relationship with her mother affected her self-esteem. Alvaro contributes with the death of his father and how worried he is about his mother. They commiserate over their parental problems, as they subconsciously inch closer to each other on the couch.

"Well," Samantha bobs her head, "It could be worse. We could be sick or criminals! Or both!"

Alvaro shakes his head, unable to escape a grim frown. Samantha kicks herself internally for making such a dumb joke, cause she thinks he's not responding well to her humor. Alvaro opens and closes his mouth several times without saying anything before Samantha realizes he's trying to gather the balls to tell her something.

"Look, there's something you should know," Alvaro scratches his head, looking anywhere but into Samantha's freckles, "My situation is difficult. I'm not really supposed to be here."

"You had a near death experience?"

"My visa...it expired. I'm here illegally."

"Oh. Well, that's okay! There's a huge community of undocumented people here! I read an article the other day that talked about-"

Alvaro is now crying. Samantha inhales sharply, taken aback. She wouldn't have noticed his tears if she wasn't staring at his face. He's not making a sound. She quickly closes the gap between them and hugs him tightly. "It's okay! It's all good, you'll figure it out," is all she can come up with. She had to stop herself from saying "**we'll** figure it out." Really, she doesn't know whether or not it'll be okay. Neither does he, which is why he's crying.

"My lawyer says I have to leave or..."

"Or what?"

"Nothing. Just that I have to leave. Once I leave the US, I'll probably be banned from coming back for a long time. No chance at a career here. I mean, I could stay, but I can't even get a job now that would sponsor me because I don't have no work authorization."

Samantha's an empathetic crier, so they sit on the couch, in each other's arms, mixing tears. Soon they are kissing. It's slow, sad, and salty.

Alvaro wakes up sometime early in the morning, when birds can be heard singing but there is no light. He wants to tell them to shut up and go back to bed. His back is sore from sitting all night. Samantha's and his limbs are entangled together on the couch. All of their clothes are on. Samantha's makeup is smeared. He studies her carefully. She really is beautiful, a girl you'd see on the street and be jealous of. How easy is her life? How much does she take for granted? Or, is she constantly bothered by aggressive guys with no filter? Does one negate the other? Her mouth is slightly open and her eyelids twitch.

Alvaro hangs his head. He chickened out, failing to mention that he was looking for someone to marry. He consoles himself, that proposing on the second date would not be the smartest of moves. He rises slowly, making sure not to disturb her. He finds a pad of paper and pencil, scribbling a note on it. Then, he rips it up, carefully discards it into the garbage, and lays down on the floor in front of the couch. He falls back asleep.

Hours later, Samantha wakes up to find Alvaro snoring on the floor below her. She stares at him, wondering if there's a future with him. Quite a lot for the first thought of the day.

She quietly takes out her phone and googles 'Ways to become an American citizen without a visa.'

She stifles a gasp as she confirms her suspicion of what Alvaro couldn't say out loud.

CHAPTER 11

Alvaro

My eyes open to find Samantha softly kicking my shoulder with her bare foot. Even her toes are perfect, painted neatly pink.

"Oh, sorry," I grunt. The image of me crying last night and spending the night on her floor slams into me violently. Mortified, I sputter, "I should go."

"It's okay," she moves toward the kitchenette, "You didn't poop yourself or anything."

"What?"

"A guy shat himself once on a first date," she continues, pulling out a carton of eggs from the fridge, "Just trying to put things into perspective."

"Appreciate that. Still, probably not the most attractive thing for me to have done."

"You're only saying this so I say that it wasn't unattractive. Which isn't completely wrong."

"That's too many negatives. I'm getting lost."

"Do you want an omelet?"

"Sure," I pull myself up onto the couch. Sunlight filters in through her partially closed blinds and mariachi music can be heard through the closed sliding glass door. I turn my gaze to Samantha. She's wearing comfortable looking two-piece green pajamas. I can tell she's wearing a bra from the way the top hangs down. Her butt jiggles as she spatulas the omelet. That's nice.

"Sorry."

"Stop apologizing."

"So-...okay."

She expertly slides a yellow mass onto a plate sitting on the counter and carries the plate to me. She raises a finger, crosses back to the kitchenette, pulls a fork from the drawer, and hands it over, before sitting next to me.

"You have to get married to stay in the country, don't you?"

My throat closes and I feel my heart start to go. There's no point in denying it. I muster a robotic up and down movement with my head.

"Well, Alvaro, I'm not going to marry you. I barely know you."

I nod again, "I didn't ask you to."

"Believe or not, I've already had several proposals in my lifetime."

That doesn't seem to be that unbelievable to me, just look at her! I keep my mouth shut, move my head in an agreeable fashion, and take a bite of egg. Good, but a little too much garlic and not enough salt. Again, keeping my mouth shut.

She goes on, "You wouldn't want to marry me anyways."

"Why not?"

She's looking red now, "I didn't tell you everything. There's parts of my job that don't really…mesh well with a traditional healthy relationship. I sell stuff on OnlyFans and do all the influencing stuff, but there's more. I'm, uhh, quite active on Seeking Arrangements and Voypure."

"What are those?"

She gives me a surprised look, "You've never heard of them?"

I actually have heard of them. I've used Voypure before, and I've had friends who've used Seeking Arrangements before, but I've never needed to buy affection. I remain silent because I want to hear her side of the story. I want to see how she explains them.

"I'm a professional cam girl and sugarbaby."

Woah. Never met one of those before. Or if I did, I didn't know. How would I have? She seems quite normal, it's hard to imagine her doing that kind of stuff. Am I disgusted? Am I turned on? Maybe a little bit of both? Puta madre.

"Cool," I muster, "What's it like?"

She nervously fiddles with the drawstrings of her pants, "It's a fulltime job. The novelty wore off pretty fast."

"Interesting."

"I can totally understand why it's a deal breaker to some."

"I don't see it as that. I don't see why that means we can't see each other?"

"You don't care?"

"Do you…um…ya know, do things with your clients?"

"Sometimes."

"Okay. That's cool," I wheeze through another mouthful of egg.

"It doesn't bother you?"

"Not really," I reply automatically. I'm not sure what to make of it really, but I'm not going to say that while I eat breakfast that she made for me.

"Great."

"I should probably get going. Thank you for letting me stay. I'll text you."

Samantha winces, "Sure. Any-...Sure, yeah."

We part ways with a hug and promise again at the door to text. As I walk to my car, I grapple with what I just learned. She's so cool, smart, funny, cute, yet I don't think I could stand being with her, knowing that she's letting other guys...ugh, I push that thought out of my head.

Does it really matter that much? I've barely just stopping fucking Annabelle. Maybe Samantha would stop that stuff if we continued to date? Camming is one thing, but sugarbabying?

When I get back to my apartment, I shut myself in my room. I pull out my laptop and phone. On my phone, I pull up my Instagram history and tap onto Samantha's profile, clicking the OnlyFans link in her bio.

On my computer, I open an incognito browser window, and enter in voypure.com. Once there, I search for Samantha's profile using her OnlyFans username. Sure enough, there it is. Six hundred and seventy thousand followers. Currently inactive. I follow it.

As I lay on my bed, I realize how intricate my ceiling is. There are all these bumps and divots. If I were microscopic, it would be a massive journey to cross it, probably more difficult than traversing any real mountain range. Alvaro, miniature explorer, conquistador del cielo! He'll traverse any surface for a small fee of three billion-

An email notification dings on my computer which lays on the bed beside me. I scramble to open the link. On my screen is Samantha. She's sitting in the very apartment I was just in. She's wearing the same green pajamas, but has taken off the bra, as I can see from the way the shirt falls. The room starts to fill with other viewers, many greeting her with thirsty messages in the public chat. A menu gets sent with a series of items. I don't have any money loaded into my account so I do nothing and watch. I feel perverted. I feel gross.

Someone pays her for *'flash tits'* and I quickly close my laptop. With the audio from the feed cut, I realize that I'm breathing hard. What is going on?

I open up the laptop to find Samantha topless. She giggles, typing furiously to some unknown viewer. I turn off the volume, face the computer away from the door, and peek my head out into the common area.

"Mahmood!? You home?"

Nothing. Still, I lock my door, pull the shades, and have the weirdest ten minutes alone I've ever had in my life.

CHAPTER 12

Alvaro

Temescal Canyon Trail is nowhere near as bad as Runyon Canyon. It's snuggled deep within the Pacific Palisades. Even though it's right off of Sunset Boulevard, the hazy Malibu coastline sucks the majority of tourists west away from the trailhead.

Plus, tripping on psychedelic mushrooms can't hurt the experience, right? Mahmood and I have met up with Alexei and Bernie for this spiritual trek.

Alexei is our Russian friend, the one who employs Mahmood at his growing weed company. Alex, as he wants to be called, is a short guy with olive skin and a square face. He also says he wants to be an actor but doesn't really seem to pursue it. Not that he needs to, he's making so much money from weed he could probably buy his way into Hollywood, something that I've seen happen. Alex's a nice guy, but his Siberian thinking doesn't do well in auditions. I would never tell this to his face.

Bernie is a ginger kid from Portland, one of my closest American friends. He worked in the Danielle Miller Acting Studio in their admin office but left for a production job shortly after I left that shit-hole. He likes to speak broken Spanish to me, which I respond to when I'm in the mood. I've actually approached him in the past about marrying me, but he's always shut it down. I get it, but these days I've considered upping my proposal payment to him. Desperate times.

Anyways, Alexei has been kind enough to provide us with the necessary narcóticos for this hike. We all grin at each other and chew the stale, disgusting fungi in the parking lot. It tastes like cardboard soaked in urine and then dried in a sock.

"Errrgh!" cries Mahmood, smacking his lips, "Give me some Gatorade! It's so gross!"

"Nobody has Gatorade," snorts Bernie, "Just wash it down with water."

"I'm going to puke! I need gatorade."

"Then go walk and buy some!"

"Calm down. Mahmood, you'll be fine. Everybody got their waters?" asks Alex, always the boss. We head up the trail, stomachs gurgling.

An hour and a half down the trail, all of our water bottles are empty. We're tromping up a steep, dusty incline with a view of Santa Monica behind us. The sun beats down relentlessly and my clothes are soaked with sweat. Nobody's thrown up yet, which is a good omen.

"You guys feel anything?" Bernie asks.

"Nope."

"No."

"Not a thing."

"Musta been a dud," Bernie grumbles, kicking a rock off the path.

A few minutes up, we come out onto a little opening off the left side of the trail where the bushes have been beaten back to reveal a breathtaking vista of the Palisades cliffs which hold up fat mansions with unused pools and tennis courts. The PCH appears and disappears in between the curving coastline. We all stop for a second, stunned by the hazy glory of it all.

"What about now?" Alexei asks hopefully.

We all shake our heads. Something shiny in the bushes over to the side catches my eye and I excuse myself to go investigate. Pushing through a brittle, dried up southern California plant, I'm disappointed to discover that the shiny thing was a wrapper for a rice crispy treat turned inside out. People suck.

The bush that I'm crouched underneath starts to undulate ever so slightly. It's flexing its arms at me. The little brown buds pulsate as if trying to communicate in some sort of code. I can't figure out what the code is, but I'm guessing if I watch it for a few more minutes, the secret will be revealed.

"Woah…"

I swing my gaze back over to my friends. They are standing in the exact spot I left them. They probably haven't moved in centuries, eons, if you really think about it. Alexei's and Mahmood's mouths are lolling open, cavernous pits of teeth and tongue. I can't see their minds through their mouths, but it all comes out there, right? It's crazy to think how versatile mouths are. We nourish ourselves completely with them, but also use them to speak and sing and spit.

Bernie's running his hand through his curly hair which embraces his hand back. Sometimes I wish I had curly hair. Oh no, did he lose his hand? Never mind. It's still there, just beyond my realm of vision, which is reality to me.

These guys would follow me to the ends of the earth and down the other side. And yet, they are just humans, like me and all the other millions of people in this city, on this coast, this continent, this globe. All just an advanced race of apes trying to make sense of existence on a chunk of rock hurtling through space. We're so insignificant, yet we worry about everything constantly.

Countries are just groups of people living in the same area who decide to agree on made up rules. They give themselves meaningless identities to protect themselves but often end up endangering themselves in the process. Mexico and the United States are fictions, inventions of people long dead and gone, but I have to base my entire way of life around their ideas. Things that really don't exist.

You know what exists? Samantha. She's real. She's a human being with her own thoughts, movements, hair, emotions, possessions, talent, and story. An evolved monkey, just like me. She may believe in the fictions that run this world, but she has to, just like me.

"Imagine, for a second," Mahmood says, pointing towards the city, "a hundred years ago, almost none of this was here."

We all look out and sure enough, one by one, the buildings start to disappear. All that is left is a luscious green and brown carpet which stretches over the horizon to the left and ends abruptly to the left with a wall of pure blue.

"Incredible," murmured Bernie. I can see tears on his

cheek. The water of despair. Alexei sits down slowly, grabbing a handful of earth, "You guys gotta try some of this…"

"It's us," I realize, nodding at him understandingly. He stares at me and with friendly confidence chuckles, "I'm not scared anymore."

"Why were you?"

"Cause of my brother."

"What did he do?"

"Nothing. That's the problem."

"What are **you** going to do?"

"What I have been doing, just with more passion. And compassion."

Mahmood, Bernie, and I all chime with agreeing grunts. It makes too much sense.

"Guys, I have something to say," I find myself announcing. They all look at me patiently, not daring to interrupt.

"I met a girl. A great one. An American one. She's beautiful and smart and creative and awesome, but she's a sex worker. I found her online camshow. I haven't seen her naked in real life, but I've seen just about everything online. I want to text her to set up another date, but I'm so frightened…frightened that I won't live up to her standards. She must have so much experience, so much sexual gracia. Should I get involved with someone like that? Won't I just disappoint her?"

"Who cares?" Alex quips, "It's her body, she can do what she wants with it. And if it goes badly, you don't have to see her again. That's the kind of world we live in."

I crouch, a much more natural position, "What happens if we get into a relationship? I don't think I can stand her fucking other guys or even knowing that other guys are jerking off to my wife."

"Maybe she'll stop," Bernie suggests, "Maybe she'll find something else if she gets into a serious relationship with you."

"I doubt it, she needs the money and I wouldn't be able to support her at all. I make way less than she does."

"So what? True love will find a way," offers Mahmood.

"Indeed," Bernie adds, cracking his neck, "Also having a super-hot girlfriend that other people fantasize about isn't really a problem."

"Thanks, guys."

I'm not really convinced, but, hell, I feel alive right now. I'm just one ape, with the power of language and science at my fingertips. There's no telling what I'm capable of.

A rogue family wearing matching LA Dodgers shirts, playing Neil Young off a speaker, invades our space, so we hike up the trail quickly. Once we're past their annoying soberness, we slow down so we can fully absorb the nature around us. We walk in silence. I contemplate my ancestors who had to walk miles for things I hardly have to think about.

My mind turns to cinema. Great art requires great sacrifice. One day, I will look back at this time and be thankful. This struggle will make me indestructible. Or perhaps, I will fall into oblivion, but a peaceful darkness that knows no problems.

By the time we make it back to the parking lot, it's dark out and our two cars are the only ones left. Alexei and I light up cigarettes which top off a shroom trip perfectly. I can only feel the dying embers of the high, small shimmerings in the air and the knocking of existential dread that comes so easily with not being on shrooms.

"That was fun," Bernie says glumly, rifling through his backpack.

"You should definitely text Sarah," Alexei directs to me, through a plume of gray smoke.

"Samantha."

"Whatever, you got nothing to lose."

"Just my dignity."

"You had that to start?"

Back in our apartment, Mahmood flops down on the couch and turns on Entourage. I sit on the floor, nursing a glass of gin. We watch Vincent Chase effortlessly pick up a girl by just smiling at her.

"God, I wish I was that attractive," Mahmood thinks out loud, "And that famous. And rich."

"It helps when a horny screenwriter is writing all your pickup lines and her replies."

"Yeah..."

The next time I look back at Mahmood, he's asleep. I switch the TV off with the remote and gently balance the plastic stick on Mahmood's forehead, using the buttons as traction on his sweaty skin. It's my way of kissing him goodnight.

I take my phone into my room and send a message to Samantha, "*Hey, how are you doing? Sorry about taking so long, I've been going through some stuff. I'm sorry about how our last date ended.*"

Almost instantly, I see her typing back. It appears and

goes away, appears, goes away. Finally, *"I'm doing okay. Don't worry about it, I get it."*

Okay, so she responded quickly, but she didn't open up any streets for more conversation. Still feeling reckless from today, I type back, *"You ever been to First Friday on Abbot Kinney?"*

"Nope."

"Wanna go with me next week?"

Typing...typing...TYPING!!!

"Sure. Can you pick me up?"

My shout wakes up Mahmood, cause I can hear the remote hit the floor. My next-door neighbor who bangs on the wall furiously. I bang back harder, giving el puto a few good "Vamos!"s for good measure.

CHAPTER 13

First Friday

They sit on a bench, munching away on their overpriced, mediocre street food. He tries to eat his Sushirrito as cleanly as possible, but the nori has been soaked by the interior sauce forcing him to tear at it with the full strength of his jaw and neck. There are rice and bits of tempura getting everywhere.

She has chosen a much wiser but much less exciting avenue, a plate of vegan tacos. Despite a greater proportion of loose ingredients, she dexterously cinches the soft shells close and turns her head almost a full ninety degrees in order to avoid any chance of facial dirtying.

The wild dichotomy of careless rich and drug-addled homeless that roam Abbott Kinney flows around them. It's the monthly First Friday fair and the madhouse community of Venice Beach has sacrificed its already traffic-filled streets to this chaotic celebration of local cuisine.

"This is pretty bland," complains Samantha, putting down the final taco.

Alvaro bobs his head, "Yeah, mine too. Sorry."

"You apologize too much for things that aren't your fault."

"I brought you here!"

"You've ruined everything!" Samantha exclaims mockingly. Alvaro rolls his eyes and pokes her playfully in the shoulder.

"Only took us forty minutes to park!"

"And twenty minutes to walk over!"

"And thirty minutes to wait in line."

"And ten minutes to find a place to sit."

Alvaro chucks the remainder of the failed fusion into a nearby trash can. He sighs, "You see yourself living in LA for the rest of your life?"

"Yeah, I don't see why not," Samantha also throws her plate away, " It can be tough sometimes, but doesn't anywhere have its drawbacks? You?"

"Not sure. When...if I make it big, I wanna get a big house somewhere abroad. Somewhere in the mountains, but also close to the coast. So you have the best of both."

"Sounds like you've thought about this a lot?"

"Maybe. Just look," Alvaro gestures across the street where a shirtless, scruffy man yells indecipherable epithets at his dog which in turn begins barking at a group of passing high school girls who quickly scamper away.

"There's crazy people everywhere."

"Yeah, but this is a pressure cooker. Nowhere else do people care more about what others think, and care so little about anybody but themselves."

Sam crossed her arms, "You know you're talking to someone who's on social media for a living? And you're trying to be an actor! You're, like, the biggest proponent of that!"

"Exactly, we're so deep in it so it's hard to notice," Alvaro juts out his bottom lip, "There's a whole world of people out there who don't give a shit about whether or not your IMDB page is long enough or which canyon your house party is in."

"Sounds like you really hate this place."

"I do and I don't. I need it, but I hate it. I'm addicted to it."

"Hmmm. I never thought about it like that. Maybe it'd be different if we were rich. This city would be a paradise if we were rich."

"Where wouldn't be a paradise if we were rich?"

They sit in silence, watching people who they'll never see again go by.

Back in Alvaro's room, they lay on his unkempt bed. He's anxious to rip off her clothes while she wants to experience things gradually. They meet in the middle, a playful push and pull.

He surprises her with skilled lips after he moves from her mouth onto her body. He knows exactly how to grab and suck her nipples. She softly bites his ear, something he didn't know he enjoys. Clothes slide off quickly.

He gets nervous, especially after his underwear exits stage left. She's undaunted and pleased. It takes a bit, but when he's there, she climbs on top while he firmly grabs hold.

"Slowly?"

"Slowly."

Of course, clear definitions of 'slowly' are not established. Alvaro gets carried away. Primal instinct takes over. Even though he's on the bottom, that's where he believes he does his best work. Samantha wants to tell him to reign it in, but it starts to feel good and soon she wants him to speed up.

She tells him and he does, furiously. Then she finds her rhythm against his thrusts. It's hypnotic, primal, and only getting faster.

It's also too much for him. He can see the crest of the hill, but he doesn't want to get there yet. He slows down which prompts her to speed up.

"Ohhh dios," he moans, which she takes as a signal to go even faster. He closes his eyes, trying his best to imagine Glenn's sweating, bald, sunburnt head.

It's useless. He's forced to release. She keeps going, spasmodically and blissfully unaware. He grabs her waist and buries his head in her bosom, hoping against all odds that her valiant efforts will keep him in the game.

No such luck. Much to her dismay, she begins to feel less of him inside her and slows to a stop, "What's wrong?"

"Nothing...nothing, I...uhhh..."

"Oh. Did you?"

"Yeah, sorry."

"No. It's okay."

"It's been a time."

She nods, kissing him softly on the lips. She's disappointed, he knows it. For the first time in years, she felt like she could actually get there with penetration. Samantha slides off, giggling at the comical pop of disconnection. They lay there, breathing hard. He looks over at her, cheeks red with perspiration, "Want me to...?"

"No, it's too sensitive right now."

They both know the moment is ruined. They stave it off

with awkward conversation for a minute. Then, Alvaro gets up to dispose of the condom which hangs off him like a suctioned half-opened Twix wrapper. She gets up to go pee, waddling to the bathroom.

They sit on the couch together, watching a cooking show on street food in Argentina. He wears sweatpants and no shirt. She wears one of his oversized t-shirts. They are sitting close to each other but not touching.

Alvaro mumbles again, "It's a compliment if anything."

"What?"

"What happened earlier. Me ending so quickly."

"It's really not a big deal. It was fun. You had fun, right?"

"If you felt the amount of stuff leaving my body, you would know that I had fun."

"Gross!"

On the screen, an old woman pushes marinated fish and fruit around a grill on a beach, speaking in her soft Argentinian accent.

Without thinking, Samantha blurts, "Something to work on."

"Work on?" Alvaro tilts his head, "Work on what for what?"

All she can hear now are alarms and high-pitched screaming. The TV screen seems to be getting farther and farther away as she is swallowed into a pit of regret. Her mind tries to escape the quickly growing hole by coming up with an excuse, but all it can come up with is a measly, "Lasting longer."

"So, you're my coach now?"

"No, no, no. That came out wrong."

"That came out wrong, like I came too wrong, too early?"

"Forget it. Never mind."

"No, I'm wondering, what did you mean?"

"Well, I just think that if we're going to be doing that more, it would be nice to build up a little stamina, that's all!"

"I see. I don't always finish so quickly, it was just...I don't know...I was excited."

They rely on the cooking show to fill the silence for a while, although neither can pay any attention to the screen.

Alvaro smirks, "But you'd like to do that again...someday?"

"How old are you? Jesus Christ, am I your first?"

"Okay, okay, I'm just self conscious. I don't know, you have sex for a living! It's like playing soccer at the park with Messi!"

"Those are two different things! When I do it with clients, I'm not enjoying myself. It's literally work for me. When I have sex for pleasure, it's supposed to be for exactly that, pleasure."

"So you never orgasmed with a client?"

"Well, no, I have, but..."

"So it was for pleasure?"

"Dude. You're making a big deal out of nothing. This is just something I do for money. You'd understand if you joined me."

"Joined you? What are you talking about? I'm not going to have sex with one of your daddies."

"No, I was referring to camming. There are couples who fuck on Voypure, but the guys can last a long time."

"Are you saying what I think you're saying?"

Samantha rolls her head back and forth, "It's just a thought. Just an idea."

"You want me to fuck you on camera?"

"On Voypure, there are lots of couples performing and they make a lot more money than solo performers!"

"And so you want me to be able to last longer so we can do shows together?"

She shrugs. He feels himself starting to get hard again. She notices the tent and grins, "Sounds like some part of you likes the idea."

"That part of me likes talking about fucking you, but going on camera in front of thousands of people is different. I don't have the self-confidence for that."

"Why not? You're fucking hot!"

"Thank you, but aren't most guys on there...ya know...I probably wouldn't **compare** to most of the other guys on there. Right?"

Samantha laughs, unwittingly devastating the last wisps of Alvaro's self-esteem. The look of dismay that appears on his face causes her to quickly backtrack, "You have no problem in that regard, trust me! Camming is not like porn. People watch cams because it's real, live, there's no tricky editing or camera angles. Plus, it's mostly about interacting with the viewers. And of course, getting them to pay the most."

"How long would I have to be able to last?"

Samantha thinks, then, "An hour or two?"

"An hour or two!?"

"What, you've never done that?"

"You've slept with a guy who could last for more than an hour?"

"Yeah, plenty of times."

Alvaro jams his pointer finger into his right tear duct, as if there's a button there to make sense of the situation, "Have you ever fucked a guy on camera?"

"Not on a live stream."

"But you've fucked a guy on camera?"

"Yes, for money. Sometimes daddies want recordings."

"Aren't you ever worried about people you know seeing it?"

"Not trying to run for president," Samantha scoffs, "I got student loans, rent, like everybody else. Plus, those videos were filmed for sugardaddies' personal use."

"You actually believe those guys are keeping these videos to themselves?"

"Let's talk about something else, okay?"

Alvaro slides off the couch, scanning the ground for his shirt, "Well, I'm sorry my sexual endurance isn't up to your standards."

"Are you fucking serious?" Samantha stands, arms on her hips, "Not what I'm saying."

"Guess my English comprehension must still be subnormal."

"I've got stuff to do today, I gotta go. This conversation is going nowhere."

"Good idea."

Samantha violently collects her belongings which are spread out on the coffee table, "I don't **want** to do this stuff. I enjoy it sometimes, not gonna lie, but it's a means to an end, just like you working at the restaurant."

Alvaro flings on his shirt, "I'm not criticizing your cooking skills and thinking that one day you'll join me at my dead-end service job!"

"I was a fucking daydream and I wasn't criticizing you! You're the one being hard on yourself! I was being nice and offering you a chance to make more money."

"Whatever," Alvaro points to the door, "Go find somebody else to fuck you on camera."

Samantha watches her own hand slap Alvaro hard across the face. She gasps more loudly than he does. Tears come to both of their eyes, his a stinging drip, hers a deluge interspersed with staccato hiccups.

CHAPTER 14

Samantha

Gerald and I look down at the shimmering blue Pacific from the inside of a rented helicopter. Including the dinner at Nobu, this will be our fourth date. The pilot tells us over our headsets that we'll be landing in a few minutes, so Gerald's papery fingers give my hand a little squeeze. I smile back, trying my best not to dread the weekend ahead.

After that fucking disaster with Alvaro, I dove headfirst back into work. Gerald had been hounding me for another date and I caved. The longer I went ghosting him, the higher the offers grew until it would be financially dumb to not take him up on his offer. On top of an all-expenses-paid weekend on Catalina Island, Gerald's paying me four grand a night.

Sex with Gerald isn't great. It's downright awful. Even though I try my best to appear like I'm enjoying myself, he must suspect something because he's graciously bought a ton of really cool art supplies which he's promised I'll be able to use all weekend. I'm hoping a few days away will clear my mind. It'll just be a few hours of discomfort.

We touchdown on a designated helipad to the side of the Catalina Airport, a tiny strip situated on a plateau with a great view overlooking the mainland. Gerald shakes the pilot's hand and helps me down from the plane. The helicopter's engine is turned off and the pilot begins unloading our bags onto the tarmac. A white Range Rover approaches and I feel like I'm about to be briefed about some covert mission for the CIA. Instead, Gerald pulls me into the backseat, introduces me to his driver Milo, a middle-aged man with an Eastern European accent. Milo gives me a knowing wink and hops out to help the helicopter pilot load the bags into the trunk.

It takes us a good thirty minutes to get to Gerald's property, which is just outside of Avalon, Catalina's biggest town.

"Here we are!" Gerald says, squeezing my thigh. I wish he'd stop touching me so incessantly. Obviously, I can't tell him to stop. Our car idles outside wrought-iron gates, through which I can see a medium sized adobe cabana with a tacky turf front lawn. The roof is redbrick and the second story master bedroom can be seen through an expansive terrace with open doors. The gates creak open and Milo glides to a stop right outside the front door. We all hop out.

"This is beautiful!" I cry dutifully.

Gerald claps Milo on the shoulder, "Please bring our bags up to the second floor."

After Milo trundles into the front door with most of our

bags balanced carefully under his arms, Gerald hugs me, "Do you like it?"

"Yes."

"Good. There's somebody I want you to meet."

What? I thought we were going to be here all alone? Maybe it's a housekeeper?

Gerald leads me into the foyer, a tall room with a staircase on the right that leads up to the second floor. Past this is an archway into a large dining room, adorned haphazardly with clashing styles of paintings, mirrors, statues. It's an interior designer's nightmare, a fucking ugly tribute to Gerald's sense of style.

Sitting at the long wooden table in the middle of the room is a handsome young guy, eating a bowl of cereal. He's tan, muscled, and blond. The nonchalant surfer look, with an innocent, pleasant face. He looks really familiar. Where do I know this guy from? USC? When he sees Gerald and me, the guy stands nervously, almost like he's been caught red-head and that he wants to run away.

"Samantha, I'd like you to meet Mitch. He'll be staying with us for the weekend. Mitch, this is my friend, Samantha."

We shake hands, smiling tentatively at each other. I can tell he's just as confused as I am. I can tell he's racking his brain to try to place me, just like I am. Gerald watches with amusement, then clears his throat, "Mitch, why don't you run into town and get us some grub for tonight? Fresh scallops? Take my card. You can use one of the carts."

Gerald hands a credit card to Mitch who scampers out the front. I hear the sound of a garage door opening and a golf cart engine puttering out onto the driveway. Milo stomps down the stairs, "I'm off! Call if you need me!"

"Thank you, Milo!" Gerald turns to me, "Most everybody on the island uses carts instead of cars. Milo lives near here year-round to maintain the place."

Okay, who cares...

The sounds of another golf-cart follows Milo's exit. I turn to Gerald, desperate for some answers, "Who is that guy? What's he doing here?"

"Mitch? He's a friend. He's been down on his luck and I thought I could cheer him up by bringing him out here with us for the weekend. Cute, eh? Do you like him?"

"How do you know him?"

Gerald grins, "Work. Don't worry, he's very nice. I'm sure you'll come to love him."

Now, I'm really freaked out. Gerald is really bad at hiding his devious glee, and I can tell Mitch wasn't expecting me to be here. Something doesn't add up. I'm guessing it'll be some kind of threesome thing Gerald's cooked up that'll most likely end up degrading me.

"I thought we were going to have the place to ourselves?"

"We do, we do! Just us three. Seriously, it'll be fun! Trust me, I've got some great plans for us. All of us," Gerald moves behind me and starts to massage my neck. It only seems to get tighter as he progresses downward. I want to scream.

Gerald snoozes on a daybed in the backyard, which is a stone patio with a small strip of green turf on one side. An above ground Jacuzzi covers the patio corner opposite of the turf strip. The daybed, a brown wicker mess with a filthy canopy, fits claustrophobically between the shiny jacuzzi and a round glass table with some rusty chairs. Milo obviously doesn't keep a very good eye on the outdoor furniture.

I'm sitting at the table, fidgeting with new paint supplies, racking my brain for answers to what the hell Gerald has planned. His translucent, pale skin is burning in the sun. I could wake him up and warn him to reapply, but I don't feel that fond of him right now. I hope he sizzles away. I hope there's just a pile of bones next time I look over at him.

Mitch steps out of the house onto the patio, holding a full grocery bag. He gives me a weak smile after seeing Gerald asleep and goes back inside. I follow him into the kitchen. Time for some answers.

"Need some help?"

Mitch nods, then opens the fridge. We start unpacking the bags. I wish he'd freaking say something. Is he really gonna make me start?

"How do I know you?" I ask, hefting what must be fish wrapped up in paper out of the bag. The refrigerator stinks of rotten food.

"Good question," Mitch squints at me, "Was about to ask you the same thing."

"How do you know Gerald?"

He bites his bottom lip, "I'm guessing the same way you know Gerald."

"Seeking Arrangements?"

"Seeking Arrangements."

"Ahh. I had no idea that he was…How long have you been with him?"

"Three months. You?"

"A month and half."

We unpack the rest of the groceries in silence. Suddenly, as I'm putting away the capers into the fridge door, it dawns on me. I know where I know Mitch from!

"You're from Chicago, right? You're a baseball player!"

Mitch smacks the countertop with an open palm, "So we have met before!"

"Yes! It was a few years ago, at Saddie's Halloween party. You were dressed as a New York Yankee! I remember because you were batting fruit that people threw at you!"

"You were the witch! Laura Goldberg's friend?" Mitch points at me, eyes sparkling with realization, "You had that wizard who kept trying to get your handle. I chased him off for you!"

"Yes, oh my god! Totally forgot about that part."

He sighs wistfully, then chuckles, "Good party. I had just broken up with Francis and you kept telling me how much of an asshole he was. I kept telling you that it was mutual, but you refused to let up. Then when he showed up, Laura put on a German accent and kept asking him if he had any meth."

"Eh, she was probably really fucked up. She tends to do those voices when she is."

"After Francis was actually cheating on me, so you and Laura had the right idea."

"I remember you asking me for advice about Seeking Arrangements."

"Yeah," Mitch mumbles, "It was good advice."

I rub the back of my neck which still hurts from Gerald's attempt at a massage. Because of my recommendation, Mitch got into the sugarbaby game. I wonder how he likes it. There's not many male sugar babies, but he definitely has the looks for it. Plus, being gay helps a lot, since most of male sugarbaby clients are also male.

"So, no more baseball?"

"Gonna try out next year for some farm teams. Just gotta stay afloat until then. Easy money, ya know."

"Yeah."

"Look," Mitch peeks out the back to check on Gerald, who's still asleep, then lowers his voice, "Tonight is gonna be...weird."

"What do you mean?"

"Gerald likes me to...he enjoys watching. If you catch my drift. He's going to ask to watch us. He's done it a few times before with me and other girls."

"I was thinking something like that was going to happen."

My heart starts to beat abnormally fast and I can feel my palms start to sweat. I can't seem to make eye contact with Mitch, but after a glance up, neither can he. We've both been paid to have sex with the other. That's not a dynamic that promotes a casual vibe.

"Wanted to let you know before it happened."

"Thanks."

In my several years of sex-work, I've never slept with a guy who was also being paid to sleep with me. I'm not necessarily opposed to it. I've been a part of three-ways and have had people watch, but never like this. I've never been choreographed like this.

After dinner, Gerald leads Mitch and I up to the master bedroom with a huge California king. The terrace doors have been left open so a warm breeze fills the room and prevents the stench of Gerald's putrid incense from overcoming my sinuses.

I'm so nervous that when Gerald sits in a chair facing the bed and asks Mitch and I to take off our clothes, my hands shake as I begin to unbutton my blouse.

"Mitch, why don't you help her?" Gerald breaths heavily.

I let Mitch remove my blouse and lower my panties. I notice a bulge in his underwear. An image of him popping some pills into his mouth and downing them with water an hour ago in the kitchen flashes in my mind. Those pills he must have taken were Viagra. I feel insulted, sad, and violated all at the same time.

"We'll take it slow," whispers Mitch. I can tell from the way his voice trembles that if it wasn't for the thousands of dollars Gerald's depositing into our bank accounts, Mitch wouldn't want to do this either. But we keep going. We're already here.

CHAPTER 15

Samantha

The Uber that Gerald bought me lets me out at my apartment. I manage to drag myself up the stairs, through the front door, and into my unit. The couch will be my bed. This past weekend was emotionally and physically exhausting. I'm ready to drown myself in weed and TV.

Mitch and I ended up having to have sex for hours both nights. Gerald must have deep pockets because both Mitch and I probably went home each with at least $15,000. Gerald just kept getting weirder and more demanding. Poor Mitch probably felt worse. He had his eyes closed for most of the time. At one point on the second night, Gerald asked me to leave the room, so I went downstairs, fiddled around with my art supplies, listened to music, and cried.

About sixteen hours after getting home, I wake to watch dawn filter into my apartment through the blinds. I'm groggy and sore. I refuse to move any of my limbs, even though my bladder is aching. Netflix is asking if I'm still watching. I click play and close my eyes.

My eyes open and suddenly it's midday. I flutter them again and it's dark again. Lovely. Might as well keep sleeping.

The next day, or maybe the day after that, I'm not really sure at this point, my phone starts to ring. I answer as I hustle to the bathroom to relieve myself. It's Laura.
"Where have you been!?"
"A trip. What's up?"
"Are you okay? You haven't been answering anything?"
"Yeah, I was with a daddy. All good."
She pauses. I can sense her fear. She thought my few days of not responding was the beginning of the end of our friendship. She's so fucking desperate and clingy. It's really off-putting. It definitely does not make me want to hang out with her.
"Are you peeing right now?"
"Yeah. What do you want?"
"Do you wanna go out tonight?"
"Ugh, not really. I'm trying to chill."
"It'll be fun," Laura pleads, "Come on, I'll text the group, we'll make it a girl's night."
"Seriously, Laura, I'm not feeling it. You're welcome to come over and watch Selling Sunset with me, but I'm not leaving my apartment."
She pauses again. She's contemplating coming over and sacrificing whatever fantastic plans she's organized for tonight.

So pathetic. She has other friends, why does she need me to be there?

"I have coke. A lot of it."

Goddammit, she's smarter than I thought.

Laura and Matilda are wearing the standard going-out-out-fits: tight dresses with heels. I've decided to throw caution to the wind and wear leggings and a t-shirt. From their sideways glances, I can tell Laura and Matilda are annoyed with my choice of attire, especially because more guys have hit on me than them since we arrived at the Den, an overpriced dive bar on Sunset. I don't even have make-up on. I think the fuckboys think that my no-fucks costume is a sign that I've lowered my standards.

Right now we're sitting in a booth bumming cigarettes off a series of rotating men, all just white noise. Laura's coke, which has made my saliva metallic, is really the only thing keeping me from leaving. Male probing questions and compliments don't register, I simply stare through them like they're phantoms with douchey collared shirts and goatees. Laura and Matilda are enjoying the attention. Good for them.

"Bathroom," I announce to Laura, demandingly. She smiles weakly and hands over her purse. The sea of Old Spice and BO parts for me as I head to the ladies' room.

A few healthy key bumps later, I examine myself in the mirror. I don't like what I see. I hate it. Nothing is left from before. Alvaro was right, this city has eaten me up. Los Angeles has sucked me dry creatively. I can't fucking paint, I don't even sketch anymore. I've become a vapid and money-obsessed fuck doll who justifies her actions by repeating over and over again: "my body, my choice, my body, my choice."

If I boil it down to the basics, and I've definitely boiled myself down to being basic as fuck, I didn't choose this way of life. My Instagram chose it for me. It connected the creeps to my page and opened the doors for the rich predators to take advantage of my poverty. My student debt and high cost of living pushed me towards easy money. I became accustomed to the lifestyle, to the constant opportunity of a quick payday. Why work a ton for minimum wage when you can send a few photos a day for thousands of dollars? Who wouldn't prefer to get paid to be wined and dined?

I'm like the worse, unsuccessful version of Frida Kahlo, known for my image more than my art. Except, I'm a sellout who doesn't paint anymore and I get my eyebrows threaded regularly.

I work a few hours a day and make way more money than most Americans, all because I'm hot. All because some guys are willing to spend five hundred dollars on a picture of my sweaty foot. The creeps and I are what's wrong with this city.

The real question is - would I be a better painter if I wasn't so conventionally attractive?

Stumbling back out into the bar, I run right into the path of a cute, crooked-smiling boy. His drunken grin fades quickly as he recognizes me. My palms drench themselves.

"Hey."

"Hey," I reply automatically, praying to God there's no white powder on my nose.

"How are-"

"Don't bother," I almost shout and brush past him, making a b-line to Laura and Matilda.

Don't look back! Don't look back!

"I'm going home," I tell Laura as I throw her purse back.

She stands and huddles near me, alarmed, "Are you okay? What happened?"

"Nothing, I'm just tired."

"Did you use all of the…?"

Out of the corner of my eye, I see Alvaro approaching. Oh shit, oh fuck!

"Hi," he says cordially, shaking Laura and Matilda's hands, "I'm Alvaro."

"What are you doing?" I spit, glaring.

"Did she tell you about me? I'm the guy that came really quickly on the second date with her," Alvaro explains to Laura and Matilda. Laura claps a hand over her mouth, stifling her throaty laugh, and Matilda blinks rapidly like she's been lightly maced.

"Oh my god!" I can't help but laugh, "You're an idiot!"

"You're right. I'm a huge idiot. An idiot who's happy to see you," he looks down at his feet, "I'm really sorry about that whole night, Samantha. I took out all my own self-hating on you."

Though his venom has been ringing around my head for weeks, I can't seem to stay mad, especially when he's pouring his heart out. Laura and Matilda stare at me in awe. I'm realizing this is probably the first time they've seen me so shaken up about a guy. I appreciate him speaking from the heart, but why does he have to do it in front of them?

"It's okay," I concede, "I wasn't being that nice either."

"Great. I'm not gonna say sorry again, cause I know you hate it," he smiles at my friends, "You guys wanna see something cool?"

"What?"

Alvaro jerks his thumb at the bar, "Ven conmigo."

Pushing through the walls of drunks, he leads us to the bar. The bartender, a portly middle-aged woman with tattoos covering most of her body, spots Alvaro and instantly moves towards him, breaking out in a knowing smile. The entire left side or the bar, all thirsty and waving credit cards, gives Alvaro a dirty look. Laura, Matilda, and I exchange bemused looks as Alvaro whispers something to the bartender who nods and flits away into a backroom.

"Do you know her!?"

"She worked at the Bloody Orange!"

The bartender returns, holding four long skinny glasses in one hand. She plops them down on the bar equally spaced apart. She begins pouring a complex series of different spirits and juices into the glasses. Half of the bar is now watching. Some are filming.

Each drink is a bluish green mixture that swirls calmly in the glass. The bartender expertly mixes four shot glasses of some sparkling orange liquid and shoots them into the larger glasses one by one. Instead of diluting the colors, orange tendrils slide onto the sides of the glass, pushing through the bluish green. I'm in awe. Is she a witch? It's like art in a glass

Alvaro bows reverently to the bartender and discreetly passes her a wad of cash. He passes the drinks to Matilda, Laura, and I. The crowd behind us quickly molds to fill in the empty space where Alvaro was. I can hear several people demanding "that drink you just made him!" but the bartender is shaking her head decisively.

"Sip it slow," he says, demonstrating, "After, watch the color."

The contents in his glass gradually darken into a rich purple. He takes another sip and it gets even darker.

"What the...," Laura mumbles.

We all take a sip. It's good, really good, a little sweet, a little spicy, with enough alcohol to buzz you but not diminish the flavor. My glass darkens, the orange receding.

"I thought you of all people would enjoy that," Alvaro beams at me.

"Yeah...thanks. Are you here alone?"

"Well, well, directly to the point."

"Shut up! I didn't mean like that."

"Roommate's with me. Where's that asshole? We were actually on our way out before I saw you. Glad we didn't, cause I'd like you to meet him."

"Where were you guys headed?"

"Saddle Ranch. Mahmood's got a date with a bull."

Laura bristles, "A mechanical bull?"

"Yes. Mahmood holds their current record, twenty seconds."

"A date with a bull means something entirely else to me," I add.

"I'm pretty good at the mechanical bull," Laura admits half-hesitantly. I'm not really sure if I heard her correctly. Matilda and I exchanged glances. In our experience, Laura's afraid to open doors because of her nails. The only thing she does at the gym is the elliptical and yoga.

We find Alvaro's roommate, a plump, tall guy with wavy brown hair and a pleasant middle eastern accent. It takes us a while of him repeating it to figure out that his name is Mahmood, not Mahommed.

Our brief ten-minute walk turns into a smoke session. Mahmood, who keeps bragging about his skills on the mechanical bull to Laura, keeps producing joints seemingly out of thin air like a Rastafarian wizard. By the time we get to Saddle Ranch, a rowdy, cheap, western-style bar, we're all high as shit.

I've never been to Saddle Ranch before, though I've seen it in a lot of people's stories. The clientele is culturally diverse and crowding the outside and inside of the restaurant. I hear at least four different languages on our way to the table. The wait staff all wear plaid shirts and headsets.

We get seated in a booth in the corner as we walk in. It's the fastest I've ever been seated in Los Angeles without a reservation. On the other side of the floor, a large circle is guarded by a wooden fence. Inside the circle is a foot of padding surrounding a mechanical bull, which is really just a half cylinder propped on its side covered in some fabric with a saddle glued on. Right now, the 'bull' is bucking gently. A big middle-aged lady topples off it. The entire place roars in drunken appreciation.

A waiter drops off a massive tub of cotton candy on our table without saying anything and sashays back away into the fray.

"He got the wrong table!" Matilda cries. Mahmood shakes

his head, ripping off a large fluff and shoving it into his mouth.

"Nah, every table gets this free."

Matilda, Laura, and I all inhale simultaneously, trying to recalibrate. Our glances share the same unspoken question. Where the hell are we?

After twenty three seconds of pretty aggressive bucking, Mahmood gets off the bull, triumphant and sweaty. Even the guy who operates the bull is clapping. The crowd is on their feet, applauding. Mahmood flounces back to our booth and bows, "It's a gift!"

"Who'd've thought a dude from Lebanon would be so good at riding a bull!" I tease. Mahmood shrugs. Laura shakes her head, a look of determination on her face.

"That was child's play."

Mahmood cocks his head, "Oh yeah? You think you can beat twenty-three seconds?"

Without a word, Laura pushes past Mahmood. Alvaro, Matilda, and I all chant Laura's name and pound the table. Laura whispers to the bull operator and enters the ring, leaping expertly onto its back. She throws her heels to the side and points at the operator who tilts his head as if to say *"here goes nothing."*

Thirty-seven seconds later, everyone is standing, cheering, high fiving each other. They whistle and scream for an encore. The DJ is yelling something indecipherable on the intercom and all the wait staff have paused to watch. Laura is standing on top of the bull, balancing with almost no effort as it bucks and spins chaotically. Her dress is hiked up a little. Matilda is posting story after story. Alvaro is slack jawed. I can't stop giggling. Over to the side, tucked into the farthest corner of the booth, Mahmood gapes.

"Did you know about this?" Alvaro askes, pointing at Laura who has extended her arms out and is pretending to surf on the bull. Even some of the valet drivers have come in to see what all the fuss is about.

"Not a clue."

"Is she from Texas or something?"

"She's a New York Jew."

Alvaro thumbs back at Mahmood, "And he's Islamic Lebanese."

"Are we writing a rom-com right now?"

"Guess so. I took a screenwriting class once."

Roughly two hours later, we're in a small room in K-Town filled with tight instrumentals. Alvaro, Laura, and Mahmood all stand with their own microphones, cords tangled in a mess on the floor. I sit over on the side with Matilda who has had one too many cocktails.

"As I walk through the valley of the shadow of death, I take a look at myself and realize there's nothing left! Cause I've been blastin' and laughin' for so long, that even my momma thinks that my mind has gone. I ain't never crossed a man that didn't deserve it, me be treated like a punk, you know that's unheard of! You better watch how you talkin' and where you walkin' Or you and your homies might be lined in chalk! I really hate to trip but I gotta lope-"

"No, no, no! Stop, stop, stop! Did you say 'lope?'"

"Yeah. Isn't that what it is?"

"It's LOC, like l-o-c. You gotta read the screen!"

"What the hell does that mean?"

"Guys, come on, we're paying for this!"

"I'm sorry, but if we're going to do this, we have to do it right. Start from the top."

"None of us are black, maybe we should pick another song…"

"Uuuuuggh, don't feel so good."

"Oh shit, I think Matilda's gonna throw up!"

"Just saying, I want us to get the lyrics right!"

"It's kind of cultural appropriation to sing this song, though, guys."

"Matilda, not in here, not in here!!"

"Laaaaarrrggg!"

"Been spending most my life, livin' in a gangster's paradise!"

"It's 'been spending most **their lives**!'"

"Get her to the bathroom! Oh god, I'm going to have to pay for their carpet…"

An hour later, we're in Playa Del Rey. Alvaro finds a tattoo parlor open at 3am. He's demanding that I sketch a goose for his shoulder. I really don't want to, because I know how much he'll regret it later, but he's being quite persistent.

"Just a goose! Small one. I know you love drawing gooses."

"Geese!"

"Whatever," he shoves a piece of paper and pen at me. The tattoo artist, a bored Asian girl with some of the best-looking bangs I've ever seen, sighs and continues to scroll on her phone from the artist chair while we argue next to her. Laura, Matilda, and Mahmood all loiter in the waiting area on two couches, chattering about what their favorite fast food place is.

"Can I record your consent?" I inquire playfully, turning my phone camera on Alvaro.

He curtsies and says something quickly in Spanish.

"English! English!"

"I, Alvaro Jimenez Rodrigo del Bosque de Maria de San Manila, consent fully and completely and all of myself to receive a tattoo of whatever Samantha draws on this piece of paper, so help me god!"

"Is that really your full name?"

"The short version, yes."

I stop the video and grab the paper. It takes me five minutes, but I'm proud of the goose once I'm done.

Alvaro hands the paper to the tattoo artist who waves him onto the chair. She and I sit on either side of the chair. Alvaro grabs my hand and grins up at me with his crooked smile. I feel like I'm about to help him deliver a baby.

"Do you have anything to numb me?"

"Here, try this," I tenderly hand him my wax pen.

The tattoo artist massages her temples, "You can't smoke that in here."

CHAPTER 16

Alvaro

My body is in so much pain.

Something heavy and warm presses my body into my mattress. It's alive! My head is pounding and I'm afraid that if I open my eyes to check, the poor little ojos will melt out of my head. I use one hand to feel the breathing lump on top of me. It's soft, shaped well, and actually smells good. Is that a boob?

"Feeling frisky?"

Samantha!

"Sorry, I'm discom**boob**ulated right now. What happened last night?"

"It was fun. We went all around. You got a tattoo that I drew."

"Really? Where?"

"Your shoulder."

"What of?"

"Take a look for yourself."

"I can't, I'm too hungover."

"Okay, no rush. It's not going anywhere. I think Laura's here."

"Here at the apartment?" I whisper, "In the room with us?"

"No. She's with Mahmood."

"Oh my. Was there karaoke at some point last night? After Saddle Ranch, I can't remember much."

I feel her nodding, her chins rubbing on my chest. Slowly, I peel my eyes open to see her beautifully mussed up face nestled on my chest. This view is worth the pain. Plus, the tattoo doesn't look half bad.

"Hi."

"Hi. Did we uhhh...?"

She shakes her head. She tightens her grip on me as if to squeeze out some sadness. I wrap my arms around her and squeeze back. She relaxes in my embrace.

"What have you been up to?" I ask, "In life?"

"The usual. Working."

"Oh yeah? Any crazy new clients?"

"We don't have to talk about this stuff. I know it makes you uncomfortable."

It does a little bit, but honestly, we had so much fun last night and when I saw her at the Den I felt relieved. I was almost hoping to run into her. Now she's in my bed with me, half naked and cuddling. "I don't care."

"Yes, you do, but it's okay."

"Seriously, I don't. If anything, it excites me.

"What do you mean?"

"Oh, just the fact that you do that stuff. You're highly desired and not afraid to flaunt it. Why would I not want what hundreds of thousands of guys dream about?"

"You don't mind that I meet up with some of these guys sometimes?"

That's definitely different. I don't like that, but maybe Bernie and guys were right. People change. Perhaps she would stop doing that if we started dating? Best not to push her too hard in the beginning.

"It does bother me a little," I don't want to plant false seeds, "but it's your life."

"I get that. Maybe I'll slow that part down, or only do non-sexual stuff."

"There's a demand for that? For non-sexual stuff?"

Samantha rubs her cheek on my chest, "Some guys pay just for conversation or pictures."

"Do they ever pay for cuddles?"

"Oh yeah. Don't worry, I already took the cash out of your wallet."

"Great. I'm going to close my eyes again."

"Can I ask you something, Alvaro?"

Uh oh. "Sure, what's up?"

"Have you ever watched my cam show?"

"I have."

"And?"

"It's hot," I confess immediately, "Extremely. I get notifications when you log on."

"I suspected as much. Why didn't you say anything?"

"How do you tell a girl on the third date that you like to watch her get naked and twerk for strangers?"

"Tell her you watch her get naked and twerk for strangers."

"I do more than just watch."

"Oh yeah? What else?"

"I could show you better than I could tell you."

Somebody knocks on the door. We both flinch. I yelp, "Who is it?"

"Samantha?" Laura murmurs through the door. I peel my eyes open as Samantha lifts her head. She grins up at me, then slides away. I try to grab her back, but she's too quick. Samantha throws on one of my shirts and cracks open the door. Laura's standing right outside of it, still wearing her dress from last night. She cranes her neck to look at me, "Can I come in?"

"Are you okay?" Samantha inquires motherly. Laura enters and sits on the edge of the bed. I cover my boxers with the sheet. I'm not sure why this has to happen right now and in my bedroom. We were just having a very nice time and I'd like to keep my eyes closed.

"Yeah," Laura turns her angry focus on me, "Your roommate. How old is he?"

"Twenty four?"

"Oh no," Laura moans, cradling her face in her palms, "Oh no! I knew it!"

"What's the big deal!?"

Suddenly, I see Mahmood getting thrown in jail or deported for sleeping with an underaged girl. His father, the high-powered ambassador, rains holy hellfire down upon the US government and Mahmood makes the front cover of every new site in the world. The two governments battle it out and send an army of investigators who find that Mahmood was living with a poor Mexican immigrant who works illegally sin papeles. I'm thrown in jail with Mahmood and we both wait on death row for years while a third World War is being fought on the outside for our freedom.

Laura must have had a really good fake ID for all the places we went last night, or maybe they never check girls? What is Samantha doing hanging out with underaged girls? I'm pretty sure they were all on coke last night...

Samantha rubs Laura's shoulder caringly, "She has this rule. She never hooks up with somebody younger than her."

My jaw and butt declench.

"Until last night!" wails Laura so suddenly that my jaw and butt reclench.

"How old are you?" I wonder if Mahmood can hear this through our apartment's paper-thin walls.

"Twenty-five."

"So only one year older than him? Why does it matter? What's wrong with hooking up with somebody younger than you?"

"You're a guy, you wouldn't understand! You're used to fooling around with younger girls, but for girls it's different. We're more mature."

"I've hooked up with older women..."

Laura rolls her eyes so hard at me that her pupils disappear for a full rotation, "I can't sacrifice my morals, Alvaro, just because you want to brag about the milfs you've slept with."

"Milfs?" Samantha gives me a stale glare.

"What the fuck! She said milfs, not me."

Laura huffs, "It's all about experience. I can't learn anything from guys who barely know their way around women."

"Well, that begs the question, how was it with Mahmood?"

Laura ponders this for a second, then, "Not bad. But that's beyond the point, rules are rules. I'm never doing coke again."

"How did you get so good at the mechanical bull!?" Samantha bursts. I sit up on the bed, eager as well to learn this. Videos of her riding the bull probably have already gone viral.

Laura shrugs, "My uncle used to run a ranch bar in Brooklyn. He used to let me use it before opening. It's a great workout."

Samantha taps her chin, "Maybe we start an exercise trend where the room is full of mechanical bulls and people have to stay on as the bulls move more violently. Could be a popular workout trend!"

"Probably just as good or better a workout than pole dancing," Laura mutters, "Anyways, this is not good. I'm sorry, Samantha, but can we go?"

Samantha chastises Laura with an icy glare and drags her out of the room. Once they've retreated into the bathroom, I throw on some shorts and peek into Mahmood's room. He's still asleep, stomach down, face buried into his pillow, one foot dangling off the foot of his bed.

Ese perro sucio.

CHAPTER 17

Samantha

I rub lotion onto Alvaro's back until the white absorbs into his tan skin. I squirt a little bit more into my hand and attack his neck, using the back of my hand to lift up his hair which is getting a little bit too long.

We're on the beach in Carlsbad, which is a little town just north of San Diego. We're on a short beach, backed by a concrete wall which is topped with a boardwalk busy with people on bikes and roller skates.

We managed to find a section of the sand not jammed with sunbathers, but since we've been sitting here, families have begun to settle closer and closer to us. The little boy of the family to our right keeps throwing his frisbee past us so he can gawk at us when he retrieves it.

There are no clouds and the sun feels really good against my skin. It's been too long since I've been to the beach. The beaches in LA are gross, not that Carlsbad's beaches are Fiji level. I pass the lotion bottle to Alvaro, "My turn."

The cold lotion on his hands makes me shiver. He massages it into my shoulders and drags some of it down onto my back, working his fingers underneath my straps.

"What is it like?" He asks, annoyingly vague.

"What is what like?"

"Being famous?"

"I'm definitely not famous. Nowhere near famous."

"That boy has thrown the disk over here five times to get a better look at you and his dad is sneaking glances at you like you're Matthew McConaughey. Then there was that girl that asked for a selfie in the store earlier."

"Well, I think the girl just recognized me but didn't actually remember from where. I'm not famous, I'm in the hazy part underneath that. As for the kid and his dad, that happened to me long before my socials blew up."

Alvaro swipes at my lower back, then hands the tube over my shoulder to me so I can finish the rest of my body off. The frisbee comes sailing over, landing onto our towel. The boy trots over and stands a few feet away, staring at my chest. Alvaro quickly gets up, grabs the frisbee, and shouts, "Go long!"

The boy flips around and sprints back down the beach. Alvaro heaves the frisbee into the ocean as far as he can. The boy comes to a stop, watching in dismay as the waves toss his toy farther down the surf. Alvaro cups his hands, "Sorry!" and sits back down next to me.

"Such a gentleman," I shake my head, giggling. My hero.

"I would like to say that I'm the only one allowed to look at you like that, but..."

"And I would like to say that I can make enough money through art to survive."

"Hey, you will one day!"

As much as I appreciate his optimism, I've come to terms with the fact that painting doesn't pay the bills. Nobody pays the bills completely through painting, not in this day and age. But I'm not going to ruin beach day with my sob story. "Thank you. I'm sure you'll be a successful actor long before I'm a successful painter."

"Who knows..." he says glumly, "I'm going to keep trying."

"You wanna go in?" I point to the water. His crooked cute grin is back as he nods. We hop up and run into the water. It's colder than I expected. He just dives headfirst into the first wave. Fucking nuts. It's too cold for that. I have to take this gradually. His head pops up a bit ahead like a seal. He barks, "Come in!"

A wave licks my upper thigh. "I don't want to get my hair wet!"

"Seriously!?"

He wades in closer to me. I can see what he's planning. I wasn't born yesterday.

"Don't you dare."

"What?"

"Get away from me!"

He circles closer, "What are you talking about?"

The bastard splashes me with water. My face is dripping. I choke, "Asshole!" then launch myself at him, pushing his shoulders underwater.

We lounge on the towel, splayed out, eyes closed. The sun

feels amazing. My foot rests on his calf. The edible has been hitting for a while now, but I'm too relaxed to go find food. I want an even tan, so it's time to roll over. Alvaro grunts and rolls over with me, "I can't wait to be famous."

"Oh yeah?"

"I mean, beyond the money, everybody loves you, wants to be around you. You can attend any show, get into anywhere, hang out with other celebrities. If there's a cause you're passionate about, you just need to record one video and everybody will donate. People just give you free shit all the time. It sounds like the dream."

"Hmmm. I guess."

"You hungry?"

"Little bit. I don't wanna get up right now, though."

"Okay. I'll look at places on Google."

Back at the Airbnb, I go into the bathroom to take a shower, but I can't get past my reflection. I'm so red all over. I had no idea. My nose is burnt and my stomach feels crispy. I didn't feel anything on the drive back. I look like a fucking lobster.

"Alvaro!"

He slouches into the bathroom, "What?"

Apparently we both should have reapplied. He's more burnt than me. The sun got his ears really badly and his shoulders look tender. He stares at me then himself. "Puta..."

"Did you bring Aloe Vera?"

He shakes his head, "What do we do?"

"Let's go to the store."

A few hours later, we're both lying on the refreshingly cool marble floor of the Airbnb kitchen. I feel like I've been hit by a train. Alvaro is dangling an empty water bottle above his open mouth. I try to regulate my breathing so I don't throw up again.

"Should we go to the hospital?" I groan.

Alvaro shakes his head, "No insurance."

"I'll cover it."

He chucks the water bottle away. I hear it skid across the floor.

"No! Please, no hospital. We just need to put on more Aloe."

CHAPTER 18

Alvaro

After a fun night out in Santa Monica, Samantha and I decide to get lunch. Last night was the first night our sunburns disappeared enough to go out in public.

As good Los Angelinos, our world revolves around going out to eat. I drive her to Canter's, a twenty-four-hour deli with a bakery in front. It's been used in countless movies, so you get a feeling of familiarity when you sit in one of the dirty boothes. She orders matzah ball soup, and I get a fried chicken sandwich.

"I want to get everything cleared up," she slurps down a sliver of soggy matzah.

"Okay."

"I really like you, and I'm pretty sure you like me, right?"

"Obviously. Are we back in high school?"

"We both have a lot of...requirements. You have your citizenship to worry about. I have my current choice of career to contend with. From what I got, the one way you can stay in the country legally and get work is by marrying an American citizen, right?"

My heart pounds as I nod.

"How long do you think that process will take? From you getting married to getting the Green Card?"

"Well, a few years, but I'd get work authorization much earlier."

"Meaning you could get jobs legally even as we were waiting?"

"Yeah."

"Okay," she puts down her spoon, "I know we've only been hanging out for a super short time, but I'm willing to help you. I'll marry you if that's what you need to get citizenship."

My mind is racing so fast it's difficult to grab specific thoughts. This would be easier when my head didn't hurt so much from a hangover. I need water and coffee and more french fries. Instead, I just look at her, saying nothing. She crinkles her nose, "I like hanging out with you. I'm happier with you than not with you, which is really all that's important, right? All I ask is that you get on cam with me. We could make a lot of money. Like, you wouldn't have to work at the restaurant anymore. We could just fuck all day."

"I don't know. This is so much."

"You don't want me to marry you?"

"No, I do, I just..."

She looks scared, like there's a knife sticking out of my head. This is it, this is what I've been waiting for all these years and I'm going to ruin it because I don't want to show my penis to a whole bunch of strangers.

I blurt, "I just don't want to show my face."

"Never. You won't have to. Guys don't really need to. I really think this will benefit us both, Alvaro. You get citizenship, you can start auditioning, and we both make a fuck ton more money."

"Alright."

What am I doing? Isn't this what I wanted? Is this the way to go about it? I definitely enjoy spending time with Samantha. She's probably the hottest girl in North America. She's giving me an opportunity to get my citizenship and tons of guilt free sex that I get paid for.

"What's the problem?" Samantha reads my face.

"I'm not sure. It all just seems too easy."

"Are you scared about the camming?"

I can't really tell if I'm scared or excited. Maybe both? Across the room, I see a group of old orthodox Jewish men munching pleasantly on their respective meals. That's what's bothering me. It's the other men of this city, paying for the love of my fiancé.

"What about the other stuff? The sugarbabying? Would you still do that?"

"Would **you** want me to do it?"

"I'll be honest, fucking you on camera is one thing, but knowing that my wife is fucking other guys is a dealbreaker."

"Fair enough. If we did this, I'd stop. We'd focus completely on camming, influencing, and OnlyFans."

She's serious. I need to warn her about what this actually is. "We're going to have to start sharing stuff, bank accounts, cars. You really gotta convince the government that you're married for real. It's not just a few years and boom. We'll most likely have to move in together. This is a huge commitment. You could get into a lot of trouble."

"Yeah, I get it. I've done the research."

"Are you still on coke?"

"No, I'm serious, Alvaro. Let's do this"

"There's gonna be interviews. Many long, grueling interviews, where they ask us really personal questions about each other. We're going to have to take a whole bunch of photos and probably have a wedding?"

"Fun!"

"Samantha, if you back out, change your mind, you'll fuck me. Not in a good way."

"As long as you help me pay off my student debt, I'll stay with you."

A waiter with blue hair and a bad case of forehead acne approaches and fills our waters. He grunts, "Anything else?"

"A slap, please."

The waiter glares at me, "Excuse me?"

"Could you please slap me?"

He trudges off with a grimace, leaving Samantha and I to contemplate the future. Samantha leans in, her hair almost dipping into the matzah ball stew, "Well?"

"Let's do it."

"Great! Shall we?"

"Shall we what?"

"Pay the bill, run home, fuck wildly on camera, and then go down to the courthouse?"

"Oh my god, right now?"

"What better way to celebrate?"

"I'd rather take a nap," I say even though there would be no way I could sleep right now.

It takes me a couple of days to gather the courage, but I know that eventually I'll have to fulfill my side of the deal. Samantha and I have been constantly talking and she's been nice enough not to press it after our brunch at Canter's. After a long talk with Mahmood, I text her to tell her I'm ready. She wants me to come over.

I drive to her apartment, accidentally running a redlight. As soon as I'm through the door, we're all over each other and practically naked in the hallway to her apartment. As the door closes, my underwear comes flying off. Samantha, naked as she is in all of my daydreams, grabs me down there and uses it as a leash to pull me onto the couch. She runs into her room and returns seconds later with her laptop and charger.

The laptop goes on the coffee table in front of the couch. Samantha plugs in the charger to the wall behind. She disappears once more, this time into her bathroom, and emerges with two towels.

"Up, up!"

I jump to let her spread the towels over the couch. I sit back down and she opens up the laptop. The screen blinds me for a second.

The little camera at the top of the laptop morphs into a black hole, sucking in all my self-confidence. The nerves begin to set in. I lose my erection.

"How many people will be watching?"

"You've watched my cam before. Probably more now that you're here."

"Yeah..."

"We don't have to do this right now. There's no rush."

"I know, I know. It's okay. Just give me a second."

Samantha gets on her knees and pushes my legs apart. She scoots in until her breasts rest on top of my groin. "You can start soft, that's fine. In fact, it's probably better."

"Maybe, we could look at some other couple's cams?"

"Great idea!"

She grabs her laptop off the table and we browse the couple cams section of Voypure.

"Wow, her breasts are huge!"

"What kind of oil is that?"

"Okay, I like that angle."

"Do you have one of those? Does it go into your vagina or your butt?"

"Traditionally my vagina, but we could get one for **your** butt."

"No, thank you. Woah, there's two girls here!"

"Look at them go."

"Oh my, he's tiny, hahaha!"

"Nah, not really, I think he's just got big thighs."

"Well, this is boring. They're just sitting there on their phones?"

"Yeah, you gotta interact with the viewers or you won't get any tips. That's why these guys have nobody watching them."

"It's really a lot of showmanship."

Samantha chortles, "Yeah, it's good acting practice."

My excitement has returned and rejuvenated my fleshy

spirit. Samantha places the computer back on the coffee table. She slides on panties and a tight shirt, "Put your underwear and shirt back on. We want them to pay to take our clothes off."

The next two hours are a slick blur. I don't really understand what is going on. Samantha's computer is dinging like crazy, each sound means more money going directly into her bank account. I've learned that once it's a simple ding, it's a small payment, usually signifying nothing but giving a slight buzz to the vibrator inside of Samantha.

Now, if it sounds like a waterfall of coins, it's a big tip. Depending on the specific amount and request, Samantha or I or both of us have to do something. I didn't really know what any of it meant, there was so much text and emojis popping up on the screen and Samantha was doing so much that I had a difficult time following along. She told me what to do and I did it.

I kept seeing people chatting about my dick and, honestly, I feel good! People were extremely encouraging and excited. I've never felt so...so big! I've always seen room for growth. I think the angle helps as well, plus Samantha's hands are pretty small. Or the viewers are just nice.

Samantha pointed out the viewer count at one point. It was hovering around three thousand! I asked if that was a lot and she said that she's never cleared that many. I asked her how much money we made. She showed me the stats of the two hours. Four thousand tokens.

"What does that mean? We made four thousand dollars!?"

"Not exactly, each token is worth five cents. So take the tokens and divide them by twenty. That's the dollar amount."

"We made two hundred dollars."

"In two hours. Hundred dollars an hour. Fifty each."

Fifty dollars an hour. Holy shit. Holy shit!!! I made twenty dollars an hour at Bloody Orange, with tips probably like thirty. I could make at least double by having sex? Wait, wait, I could make double by having sex with my sexy American wife? Is this what they call a big break?

Even more impressively, I had the endurance to last forty-five minutes the first time and an hour the second time - back to back! I can tell Samantha was pleased. We're sitting on her couch smoking a joint, showered but still naked.

"Had fun?"

"Too much. What did you think?"

"I think you're a natural. For a bit, we were on the leaderboards."

"Leaderboards?"

"Each hour, they list who was the most watched cam on Voypure. We made the top ten."

"Woah."

She smirks, "You've got the body, Alvaro. Use it."

"As long as I never show my face."

"Sure thing, Mr. Chalamet. Let's take some photos for OnlyFans."

"Uh, okay, what do I do?"

"I'll need you to get- never mind, you're already there!"

"It's easy when you're not wearing anything!"

Samantha opens her phone camera and takes a series of selfies from different angles, all involving my you-know-what.

She squeals between shots, "This is so much more fun when I have a prop!"

It goes from static shots to short videos. These eventually get longer and more involved until we're at it again for the third time today. We pass her phone back and forth, getting more and more creative. Sexual guerilla cinematography.

"Wait, wait, wait, don't cum yet! You gotta get it on my chest!"

Against all odds, I'm able to pull out and spray over her chest.

"Got it!" cries Samantha and stops the recording, "God, that was hot."

"I'm surprised I still had any left. I need another shower and a nap."

"We're going to make so much money on all of these."

"Yeah?"

Samantha giggles as she scrolls through the pictures and videos that we just took, "Way more than Voypure."

"What are we talking about here?"

"Camming is really just to build a bigger fan base. I make most of my money on OnlyFans. Probably make ten grand a month."

Ten grand a month. Ten grand a month. Twelve months of ten grand a month. A hundred twenty thousand dollars a year. And that's what she makes now. Even split between two people, it's hard to believe. I'm looking at minimum, sixty thousand a year for some racy online shenanigans. No wonder she does this. Why wouldn't any hot person do this!? It's so easy.

I must look like I'm having a stroke. Am I?

CHAPTER 19

Samantha

"You can't seriously be considering this?" Laura cries, scrutinizing me with full force. I have just broken the news of my decision to marry Alvaro, which I may have done too bluntly. I can see the veins on Laura's temples bulging.

"Why not?" I counter, "I like him, like, a lot."

We're sitting in my hot tub, towels at the side, readying us for a prompt exit if any of the other tenants in my apartment decide they need to join us.

"Isn't it super illegal? What happens if they suspect this marriage is a sham?"

"Laura, relax! Alvaro and I have discussed this a ton. We're going to date for at least three months before doing anything. It'll help us for the interviews and look less suspicious, you know, it would be weird to get married after a few dates."

"Listen to yourself! You literally just told me you're getting married to **this guy who you've only been on a few**

dates with! You're, like, scheming on how to trick the system. Couldn't you go to prison for this?"

"So many people do this. It's really not a big deal."

"Do you really like him that much?"

I nod enthusiastically, "Yes!"

"Wasn't he a little **impatient** in bed?"

"That was one time. We've already cammed together a few times and he's improved, like, a lot. Our viewers skyrocketed. I can see myself actually making the account a couples one for real."

Laura rubs her veins in a vain attempt to get them to recede. She's trying to formulate her takedown, but all she comes up with is a weak jab, "He's a waiter, Sam."

"So? He can't get a better job now because of his citizenship status. Once I get him the Green Card, he can do a lot more. And now he's a cammer, like me."

"And what does he want to be?"

"An actor."

"Sam..."

"Look, it's really not that big of a deal. It'll take a few years, but we're both getting something from it. It'll benefit both of us."

She shakes her head at me with her east coast exasperated noises, which I know is tinged with jealousy. I turn the interrogation on her. "What's going on with you and Mahmood?"

"Ugh, I do **not** wanna talk about him."

"Was it good? You never answered. I know you've been hooking up with him."

"Yeah," she admits, sheepishly, "I don't know. He's not my type. I'm just bored. It's never gonna work."

"Cause he's younger than you?"

"He's a Muslim!"

"Laura!"

"No, no! You wouldn't understand, your family's not Jewish."

"Mahmood smokes weed all day. He's not a devout Muslim. He has Entourage posters all over his room."

"I know. That's not a good thing."

I giggle, "Totally!"

She crosses her arms, pouting, "Well, I'm not going to marry his crazy ass."

"Wouldn't want you stealing our thunder. Leave all the cute immigrant husbands to me!"

My phone starts to ring. I quickly dry off my hands and examine who it is. Dad. I flash the screen to Laura who nods and puts a finger up to her lips. I slide to answer.

"Hi Dad."

"Sammy! How are you doing, honey?"

"I'm good, I'm good. Just sitting in my hot tub. You?"

"Great, just don't spend too much time on it. It can be really dehydrating. They say you should only spend at maximum twenty-"

"Did you call to lecture me on hot tub etiquette?"

"No! I'm calling to ask you when you're having your next art show?"

Oh god, not this again!

"Ummm, probably in the next few weeks. Why?"

"Do you have an exact date in mind?"

"Not yet. That's not really how these things work."

Laura sniggers. I flip her off.

"I only ask because your mother and I have decided we want to come visit you! We'd love to go to one of your shows while we're there!"

"What?"

"We're coming to visit! Can you hear me alright? This damn phone, did I mute myself?"

It's a good thing I'm in a pool because I can just dip my sweaty hands into the water, but I'll have to dry them off to touch my phone. What the fuck is going on? When did my parents become loving and financially stable enough to come visit their only daughter?

"Um, really?"

"Yeah! I feel bad we haven't visited you, Sammy. It's just money's been tight and-"

"I don't think I have enough room to keep you guys in my apartment..."

"No worries at all!"

"Hotels are pretty expensive out here. You know, maybe I could fly out there, it's been a while since I've been home."

"It's all good, really. We're going to stay with Aunt Millie!"

Aunt Millie. I totally forgot about her. Aunt Millie is an old childhood friend of my dad. She's not really an aunt, but we always used to call her that. She works HR for some shipping company out in the Inland Empire, if I remember correctly. I recall my mother not liking her very much. I didn't mind her. She used to come over to our house on Sundays and play Scrabble with me. She always smelled like cat pee. When I first went to USC, she tried to get me to come out to her house, but I didn't have a car.

"Doesn't Aunt Millie live super far east?" One final attempt at dissuading my dad.

"It's a thirty-minute car ride! I routed it on Google Maps!"

"Yeah, that's thirty minutes now. During rush hour, that's two and half hours."

"Well, that's what podcasts are for! What, you don't want us to come out?"

"No...I would love for you to come out."

"Great! We've already bought the tickets. We're flying in on the 5th and leaving on the 14th. Could you schedule your show for some time then, please? It would mean the world."

"I don't know, it's hard to nail down venues this close in advance. I'll let you know."

"Please, Sammy? You never want to send us anything and this will be the one chance we'll get to see it in person."

"Okay. I'll try my best."

"Thank you, sweetie. I'll text you later! Can't wait!"

"Me neither, Dad."

"Love you, Sammy."

"Love you too, Dad."

I chuck my phone into the swirling, boiling liquid. Laura squeals and tries to kick it up while keeping her hair dry. I'm so screwed.

"Sam! Your phone!"

"Do you know anybody with a studio space?"

"Okay, it's your phone, you can get it."

A family with two kids enters the hot tub area, eyeing us cautiously. It's time to leave. Laura and I climb out, quickly wrapping ourselves in our towels.

The next day at the Apple store, Ron gives me a stern lecture, "Young lady, you can't keep bringing your phone into the water with you! This is costing you too much! You come back here again for a new phone, I won't give it to you!"

I take the new phone and pocket it, smiling warmly at Ron, "Do you know anybody with studio space?"

"Huh? Listen, young lady, you need to be more careful with your finances. This is because I care about you. Was it a boy again this time?"

"Not a boy, just a fat lady and my dad. Have you ever disappointed your parents, Ron?"

Ron shakes his head, "Both my parents were murdered by Turkish soldiers. I barely remember them."

"Oh my god, I'm so sorry. Thank you, Ron, I promise I won't drop my phone again."

Ron shrugs and I slink out.

CHAPTER 20

Alvaro

For the staff of the Bloody Orange, tonight's been a shitshow. There's even a line out front, which usually doesn't happen. We've been trying to limit people to an hour at their tables, but we can't really kick them out or we'd face the wrath of Yelp.

Wilzon had the bright idea to let people in line order drinks, but it kind of backfired. Patrons are getting crazy. There was already a fight between two guys about a girlfriend's butt being grabbed. Some other dude decided to take a pee on the valet stand and got thrown out by Jake and Randal.

My section's been more hectic than usual. I've been watching this one table full of rednecks slowly disappear. One by one, they've been "going to the bathroom" and never reappearing. I'm absolutely sure they're trying to dine and dash. Only two are left. They keep watching me and whispering to each other.

"Can I get you two anything else?" I run up to the table.

The two dudes, one fat with a red trucker hat and the other wire thin with a poorly shaped goatee and mullet, exchange nervous looks. Red Trucker grunts, "Can I get another screwdriver?"

"Of course," I catch Annabelle by the shoulder and tell her the order. She gives me a pained glance and scuttles off towards the kitchen. The two hillbillies grimace, most likely thinking that that extra order should have gotten me away from their table.

"Anything else?"

"Yeah, get me one of those hummus plates," Goatee requests gruffly.

I rotate my head faux-sorrowfully, "Kitchens closed, unfortunately."

Just as I say this, Mildréd, an older Peruvian waitress, arrives at a nearby table with a platter full of food. The rednecks look at her and then back to me. They know I know. We stare at each other hard. Sweat pours down their pasty skin. We all tense. Time starts to slow.

Then, they're on their feet and dashing through tables. They bump a table with a hookah on it. The large glass structure tips and shatters. Wilzon is yelling. Patrons duck their heads and scramble to hit record on their phone cameras. Jake and Randall crack their knuckles and step in the middle of the front entryway. Red Trucker smartly vaults over the side and lands with an impressive roll. He must do some sort of redneck parkour. Goatee tries his luck with Jake and Randall, probably thinking he can barrel through them if he gets enough speed. He's been watching too much American football. He's slammed into the front steps with so much force that he bounces back up into a nearby metal railing. A collective 'ooooooo' reverberates throughout the Bloody Orange and Jake dials for an ambulance as Randall checks to see if Goatee is still breathing.

"Watch your fucking table better," Wilzon spits angrily at me after he calls me over to the bar, "You should have seen that way earlier."

"En serio?"

"Yeah, that's the third time this month somebody's tried that in your section. It'll start coming out of your paycheck."

"Am I supposed to accuse them of dining and dashing before they've done it?"

"You're supposed to tell me when you suspect anything."

"Si, jefe."

"Do better, you've been here too long for that shit to happen," Wilzon disappears into the kitchen like an angry ghost.

After another hour, I'm smoking a joint on my break a street above Sunset when Annabelle strolls up. She sits next to me and plucks the joint from my lips. She inhales a near third of it.

"You okay?"

I nod. She smells like crab cakes. Why is she being nice?

"Where have you been?"

"What do you mean?"

She hands the joint back to me, "You haven't texted me in forever."

"I'm with somebody."

"So am I."

"Nice. With who?"

"This guy Charlie. We met in my spin class."

"How long have you guys been seeing each other?"

"About a month."

"If you're seeing someone, why would you care or not if I texted you?"

"Alvaro, you're like the horniest person I've ever met."

"So? What does that have to do with you?"

Faster than I expected, her hand is on my lap. She's grinning, "You're telling me you don't want to fuck tonight?"

I firmly grab her wrist and wrench it off of my jeans, "That's what I'm telling you."

She pretend-pouts, "Wittle Alvaro's in wuve!"

"I feel sorry for Charlie," I stand, sucking one more time on the joint.

"Not as sorry as I feel for whoever you tricked into dating you. Does she know yet that you're only in it for the Green Card?"

"She does, actually. We're gonna get married. Does Charlie know his girl puts the horns on him, or is he cheating on you and this is your way of getting revenge?"

Annabelle's face falls for a split second before she regains her haughty composure, "I'm just fucking with you, asshole."

"My break's over," I flick the half-burnt joint into a trashcan and head down the hill towards Sunset.

"You both must be batshit if you think this a good idea!" she yells after me. I can't come up with a snappy reply, because maybe she's not wrong.

"This is not what I ordered," repeats the lady with no

eyebrows. I look at my notebook and what's on the table. It's the same thing, zaatar bread. She's already eaten half of it.

"Yes, it is," I point at the menu.

"I'm telling you, it's not what I ordered. Isn't the customer always right?"

"You've already eaten half of it. Why didn't you say anything when I brought it out?"

Her husband or brother or father or uncle is a tired-looking fogie with a horrible hairpiece. He sits across from her, unvexed by the scene she's making, contently puffing away on hookah. The lady with no eyebrows would look madder if she had some hair above her eyes to accentuate her emotions. She just looks like she's trying really hard to poop.

"I was embarrassed for you," the lady fumes, "I also didn't realize what had come out."

"I think you just want a free meal."

"Excuse **me**!?"

Fuck this. Fuck this woman. Fuck this job. Fuck Wilzon. I don't need it. I can make way more money with Samantha. I could be fucking Samantha right now and be making more tips that anybody at the Bloody Orange. Wilzon and Annabel and this lady with no eyebrows can go drown in their boring, pathetic, prude lives.

"We both know that you ordered this. Judging from your boyfriend's or brother's lack of reaction, you do this all the time. It must work if you're doing it now. I've just had a long night and I'm done with bullshit."

The lady with no eyebrows starts to choke on her words, her zaatar, I'm not sure. Her husbandbrother finally begins to grow concerned at seeing her unable to screech.

I point to the zaatar, "If you're not going to pay for that, I'll eat the rest of it. I'm pretty high and could use some munchies."

"Alvaro!" Wilzon is standing by the table now, hands on his hips.

"Jefe, why don't you suck my dick?"

"Out! You're fired! Get out!"

The lady with no eyebrows is wailing now. Patrons and most of the waitstaff are watching. I shrug and sit down at the lady's table, pulling an empty chair from another table. I start munching on the zaatar. It's quite good. Wilzon has joined the lady with no eyebrows in staring at me in pure disbelief. Jake and Randall are making their way over.

"Can somebody get me more hummus? The garlic hummus, please," I ask through a mouthful. I beckon for the hookah pipe. The husbandbrother hands it to me without thinking. After taking a huge puff, I blow the purple smoke out hard, so it billows into the rafters.

CHAPTER 21

Fucking Star

Sam and Alvaro are camming on Voypure in Samantha's apartment. At this exact moment, he's in her mouth, a request brought on by a waterfall of tips. Somebody keeps tipping for 'keep going' which means Sam and Alvaro are supposed to keep doing what they're doing. No complaints.

Alvaro taps Samantha's hip, a signal that he's getting too close. Can't blow before you're paid or the viewers will be mad, something Alvaro had to learn quickly and early. In response to his tap, Samantha ceases using her tongue and releases pressure from her lips.

Before either has a chance to breathe, somebody pays for the tip 'cum on face.'

"Thank god," murmurs Alvaro.

He stands and positions the camera so the viewers see a close up profile of Samantha. She smiles at the camera and then up to him. Tips are pouring in so fast that the vibrator inside of her is exploding. Suddenly her knees are weak.

Alvaro massages himself until he releases. The chat moves too fast to read. Their viewers count skyrockets. Samantha turns to fully face the camera, tilting her face up ever so slightly.

Half an hour later, the show is over. Alvaro rests on the couch, flipping through Sam's sketchbook. Sam is on the floor reviewing over the stats from the show. She squeals in excitement.

"What?"

"We made it to number one! For the last hour, we made more tips than any other cammers on Voypure!"

"Woah. How many?"

"We had eleven thousand people watching our cam at one point."

"Puta madre," Alvaro closes the sketchbook and joins Sam on the floor, examining the screen thoughtfully, "How much did we make?"

"A grand. But that's not even the best thing," Sam opens up her email and pushes the laptop to Alvaro who squints at the screen. There's a long message written with impeccable grammar and formality.

"I don't understand. Who's Daniel and Danielle?"

"Only the greatest camming couple of all time!" Sam grabs the computer back and deftly pulls up a video of two beautiful people having sex. The man is dark and lanky, with curly black hair. The woman is petite and curvy with blonde curly hair. He's sitting down on a couch, facing the camera while she sits on him, her legs draped over to one side. They're at it, hard.

"Oh, wow," Alvaro breathes. Sam clicks another video

and it's the same couple, but this time with a slender middle eastern girl.

"They do threesomes and foursomes a lot," Samantha remarks with a heavy admiration, "They're crazy. They use toys and do all sorts of stuff. But it pays off, they have the most followers of any other account. I think I heard Danielle charges six hundred for one photo on OnlyFans!"

"And they want to work with us?"

"Maybe. They want to set up a phone call, probably like an interview, to see what we would be comfortable with."

"And you think we should do it?"

"It would expand our fanbase by so much. All their fans would be exposed to our camroom. Their clout would trickle down to us."

Alvaro scoffs, "You make it sound like they're gods."

"They kinda are," Sam pauses, "You might have to show your face, though. I think everybody who goes on their show shows their face."

"Aaah. I don't know. Feel like I shouldn't sacrifice that."

"It would mean a lot more money."

Alvaro nods and looks at his feet. Samantha immediately clarifies, "Why don't we set up a phone call with them and if they need you to show your face, we can decline?"

Alvaro blushes, "I guess, but it's not really just the face thing. I've never even had a threesome before."

"You haven't?"

"Nope. Not everybody's as experienced as you."

"Hey!" Samantha pouts, "Mean."

"Sorry, not like that! All I'm saying is that I'm not sure

how I feel about watching you get fucked by some other guy. How's that any different from the sugarbaby stuff?"

"Cause I wouldn't be getting fucked by the guy paying."

"I don't see any real differences."

Samantha cracks her neck by leaning side to side, "You'd get to fuck Danielle."

"I don't really want to fuck Danielle."

"Oh, come on," Samantha pulls up the video of Danielle and points bluntly at the screen, "You're telling me you wouldn't want to fuck her?"

"You realize that we're practically engaged?"

"Keyword, **practically**. Meaning it's practical."

"Great," Alvaro concedes dryly, "We'll set up the call, but I don't want to do it if I have to show my face."

"Okay."

"Okay."

Samantha stands, trying her best to ignore away the tension, "I need to work on some stuff for this show. If my parents figure out I'm not actually living off art, I'll be disowned."

"Why not tell them the truth?"

"Uh, would you tell your mom what you're doing?"

Alvaro shakes his head, "Your parents aren't crazy devout Catholics like my mom."

"My parents are just crazy crazy. Especially my mother."

"Am I going to meet them?"

She freezes. This unprecedented realization washes over her, drenching her palms. Slowly, Sam stutters, "Y-You want to meet them?"

"We're gonna be married, remember? Might as well."

"Fine, but I'm gonna have to prep you."

He cracks his knuckles, "Bring it on!"

CHAPTER 22

Las Sugarbabies

Caroline's Aunt's massive minivan barrels down the highway at relativistic speeds. Caroline drives and sneaks peeks at her phone, much to the annoyance of Kimberly who sits in the front seat. "Look at Reddit one more time while you drive," threatens Kimberly, "and I'm throwing your phone out the window."

Mahmood snores in the passenger-side middle-row seat by the sliding door, his long legs crushed up against the back of Kimberly's seat. Samantha sits on Alvaro's lap on the driver-side middle-row seat. Alvaro's lower half has gone to sleep but he doesn't have the gall to say anything.

Bernie, Laura, and Matilda jostle each other for space in the back row. Bernie keeps hitting his nicotine pen and trying to blow it out of the cracked-open window, but it keeps blowing into Laura's face. Matilda is watching Handmaid's Tale on her phone, definitely the most content in the car besides the unconscious Mahmood.

It's almost nine at night, so darkness pervades everywhere but the van's headlights which show the highway zooming underneath them. Caroline squints down the road at the horizon, barely discernible from the inky night sky, "Woah, what is that?"

Kimberly peers forward, "What's what?"

"That light? In front of us?"

Samantha wiggles on Alvaro's lap excitedly, "That's Vegas!"

They shoot over the crest and come into full view of Sin City. Even Matilda puts her phone down to gape. Alvaro kicks Mahmood out of his slumber.

Samantha whispers in Alvaro's ear, but everyone hears, "How many times have you gone to Vegas?"

"A few times. Maybe once every three years."

"Vegas is, like, the sugarbaby heaven."

"The sugarbaby mecca?" chimes in Mahmood.

"The great city of sugarbabies?" adds Kimberly in a British accent.

Matilda quips proudly, "Simp city?"

"I'm not joking," Samantha giggles, "You'll see."

Caroline glances at them through the rearview mirror, "I thought it was Dubai?"

"Vegas is the American sugarbaby capital."

"I don't think anybody doesn't believe you," Alvaro grunts, bouncing his legs slightly to wake them up, "Sugarbaby heaven is a hilarious image."

"I think we're actually in time for the annual conference!"

"Vegas, Vegas, Vegas, Vegas, Vegas, Vegas, Vegas, Vegas, Vegas!"

Matilda's father got them a penthouse at the top of Resorts World, one of the newer goliaths that pepper the Las Vegas Strip. Three massive towers unite in the middle. Technically, it's three hotels, the Hilton, the Conrad, and the Crockfords, but it's all connected to one giant gambling floor and faux-Asian food court. Even if they had split the penthouse eight ways, it would cost at least a grand per head. God bless Matilda's father's money.

Upon walking into the cavernous luxurious suite, Alvaro, Samantha, and Bernie, the resident "poor kids" of the group all gasp, then smirk at each other in the collective realization that it's awesome to have rich friends.

Laura, Matilda, Caroline, Kimberly, and Mahmood all seem unimpressed, like every hotel room they stay in has twenty-foot-tall ceilings, a dining room overlooking the Strip, four bedrooms, two and half baths, a jacuzzi, a game room with billiards, a hundred-inch television screen, a fireplace, a fully stocked kitchen, a balcony with a grill, and an elevator that enters directly into the room.

Room designations are quickly made. Alvaro and Samantha, Laura and Matilda, Caroline and Kimberly, and Bernie and Mahmood. There's little fuss over choices since each room has a king-sized bed. As everybody unpacks, Bernie covertly sneaks into the elevator and is gone.

"Where did Bernie go?" Sam asks Mahmood in the living room. Mahmood shrugs, extracting a joint from his fanny pack.

"Probably on the floors already. He's a big gambler."

Kimberly saunters in and fixes a vicious glare on

Mahmood's joint, "Go out to the balcony if you're going to do that!"

Mahmood hops up, "You want to join?"

Kimberly tuts disapprovingly but she moves towards the open balcony doors as soon as Mahmood steps into the dry Vegas night. Alvaro and Samantha sink into the couch, tangling their limbs together like some fleshy pretzel. Caroline, Matilda, and Laura come in from their bedrooms to join the couple on the couch and start tittering about the night ahead.

"This weekend is going to be crazy," Alvaro whispers to Samantha. She kisses his cheek. Laura rolls her eyes and proclaims loudly, "I'm going to throw up if I have to watch you two be all gross and togethery. Can we make a no-sex-outside-the-bedroom rule?"

"We can't promise that," Alvaro shoots back.

Samantha reddens, "Alvaro!"

Laura glowers when she spots Mahmood passing the joint to Kimberly outside. Everybody notices this and breaks out laughing. Laura storms off to her room.

"I thought she didn't want anything to do with Mahmood?" Alvaro muses.

Samantha rolls her eyes, "Laura's the kind of person who says everything that she doesn't mean. Once you figure that out, she's easy. If you want her to do something, tell her to do the opposite."

"Makes sense."

Caroline scoots to the edge of the couch, demanding the room's attention, "Let's go to dinner, I'm starving."

"Seconded!" cries Mahmood who just popped in from the

balcony with Kimberly. Both of their eyes are red and half-lidded. Samantha plugs her nose teasingly.

Matilda rises, dusting off the front of her dress, "I'll go get Laura."

Alvaro pulls out his phone and calls Bernie. It goes straight to voicemail. All seven of them crowd into the elevator. As the doors slide shut, a muffled, "Vegas! Vegas! Vegas!" echoes up and down the elevator shaft.

The hostess leads the five girls and two guys through a crowded chic Chinese restaurant. All the other patrons are either old and rich or young and attractive. Sam and Alvaro's group fit into the latter, so they blend in perfectly. There are no families.

The hostess gives them a large round table in the center of the place so they can be seen by all. She smiles, distributes menus, and vanishes. Sam notices Laura makes sure to sit on the opposite side of the table from Mahmood.

In the back of the restaurant, another waiter opens a door that leads into a backroom in which scores of large, hairy men drink loudly like Vikings after a successful raid. Everybody glances over at the noise. Alvaro sees Samantha take on the same meek look she had when they went to the bar near UCLA and got uncomfortable with the guys already there. He carefully studies the men. They're all huge, physically and socially, brimming with confidence. Some of them have crooked noses and are missing teeth.

Alvaro watches as one of the Vikings glances out the open door back out at their table and immediately fixates on Sam.

Sam realizes Alvaro's watching all of this and claws at his thigh desperately, blurting, "What are you going to get?"

"Not sure. Probably just drinks."

A few of the Vikings strut out of the backroom towards their table. Laura, Matilda, Caroline, and Kimberly all straighten their posture while Samantha hunkers down. Alvaro and Mahmood give each other perplexed looks.

"Samantha, baby!" cries the lead Viking, a barrel-chested, bearded specimen with a nose that slants right halfway up, "Been too long!"

Samantha returns him a cold nod. The Viking chieftain pauses, taking in Alvaro's proximity to Sam and grins. His buddies snicker as he glides to Sam's side, opposite of Alvaro who at this point is clenching his fists tightly underneath the table.

"How's everybody doing?" The chieftain addresses the entire table. He's close enough to assail them with the putrid stench of BO and whiskey.

"Fuck off," pipes up Laura. Everybody, including Samantha, looks at Laura in surprise.

"Excuse me?" the barbarian starts to move towards Laura, "What'd I do to deserve that?"

"Just leave us alone," mumbles Laura, much less confident now that he's focusing on her.

"Your friend Samantha and I have a little history, did y'all know that? We used to hang out a lot. A lot, a lot."

Samantha's hand finds and envelopes Alvaro's fist. She prays to all the Gods she doesn't believe in that this stupid arrogant hockey player would just leave. Or, at the very least, not recount what he had paid her to do.

"We had too much fun, didn't we?" The predator continues to circle his prey, eyes locked onto his old conquest. He breaks his gaze to turn to one of his henchmen, "Got a hundred bucks? I'm in the mood for a quick fuck."

Alvaro explodes out of his seat. Samantha and Kimberly scream. The Viking calmly side-steps Alvaro's poorly timed lunge and trips him. Alvaro spills onto the floor, taking down an unfortunate passing waiter holding a tray along. Mahmood is on his feet, but Laura is quicker. She gets in between Mahmood and the Viking who laughs and skips towards the backroom, his followers on his tail making faces and rude gestures as they go. The girls and Mahmood all help Alvaro and the waiter get up to help.

"Are you mad at me?" Alvaro says from the cushioned seat at a slot machine on the casino floor.

Samantha sits in the adjacent seat, clutching her purse to her chest, "You shouldn't have tried to fight him."

"I was defending you! He was being a complete asshole."

"Yeah, but that doesn't mean you have to attack him!"

"What should I have done?"

"I don't know, **ignore** him. He was feeding off your reaction."

Alvaro spins slightly in his chair, "He would've just kept going. He was a client?"

"Yeah. Early on. I was clueless and kind of blinded by his blue check mark. He got borderline abusive, so I stopped responding."

"You said he's on the LA Kings?"

"If that's the hockey team in Los Angeles, then yes."

"Puta mierda."

"You're gonna have to get used to stuff like that. That's just what our profession brings."

Alvaro deflates, "I can't believe I'm getting in trouble for trying to defend you!"

"Dude!" Sam jumps into his lap, making the chair spin them around, "My entire life is a fight between my dignity and my personal safety. I can stand some drunk asshole berating me, that's what I call a Friday night! What I won't stand is my fiancé in the hospital because he tried to fight a professional hockey player at a restaurant in Vegas! Right?"

Alvaro stares at Samantha for a full ten seconds before he hiccups and quickly covers his mouth, "You're always right. I'm a dummy."

"But you're **my** dummy!"

"Wait, look over there!" Alvaro spins the chair and points to a roulette table about thirty feet away. Bernie, looking quite haggard, is leaning over the roulette numbers, spreading chips around. Sam and Alvaro get up and walk over to him.

"Bern!" Alvaro claps his hands on his friend's shoulder, "Where ya been?"

"Here, there, everywhere," grumbles Bernie without looking up from the table. The croupier, a bored Filipina holds up her index finger and thumb, "IDs."

Sam hands her ID and Alvaro hands over his passport. Bernie spreads two hundred more dollars in fives around the table. The croupier passes the IDs back and spins the ball. Alvaro and Sam sit on either side of Bernie who impulsively moves fifty dollars on red. The croupier waves her hand over the table, "No more bets!"

"What are you at, dude?" Alvaro asks gently. Bernie ignores him and bites his nails manically. The ball lands on 4 black. No chips on it. The croupier smugly swipes away all the chips. Bernie loses everything, but he doesn't even seem to register, just starts fingering more chips.

"How much are you down?" asks Alvaro, this time with a little more assertion. Bernie flips around angrily, "A few grand, okay!? Who are you, my fucking mom?"

"Come on, Bernie," Samantha coaxes, "We're all going to go see Diplo at the Wynn. Take a break, the tables will be here."

"Nah, why would I wait in line to see a DJ? I'll find you guys later."

"You hungry? You weren't at dinner. Alvaro got into a little fight. It was pretty crazy."

Bernie flips around, a massive sarcastically-wide smile plastered underneath dark bags, "I'm good here, but you go have fun. Thanks for checking in! Are you okay with that?"

"Not really."

"Well, I couldn't give two shits about what you are okay with or not. I don't even know you. You're just some girl fucking my friend."

Samantha blinks, offended, "Alvaro, do you hear how your friend is talking to me?"

Alvaro hops off the stool and squeezes Bernie's shoulder once more. Bernie slaps his hand away. The pit boss strides over, crossing his broad arms together. Alvaro leads Samantha away.

"Lesson learned, I'm not going to fight anybody for you."

"That's not what I meant. He's your friend, you can fight **him**."

Sam, Alvaro, Laura, Matilda, Caroline, Kimberly, and Mahmood stand in line in a gaudy, Victorian style hallway. It's still inside the casino, so Vegas tourists pass by in their shorts and Hawaiian shirts on the outside side of the red rope. Inside the red rope, all of the young partiers are dressed like they're trying really hard not to try to look like they spent the last few hours filling their phone storage with mirror selfies.

Sam and Alvaro's group wait twenty minutes and make it past the first checkpoint purely on their girl to guy ratio, a healthy five to two. They each get a green paper bracelet around their left wrist. They enter into another line in a dark corridor with mirrors on either side. The parallel reflection causes dizzying endless feedback loops magnified with selfie-flashes. Caroline, who suffers from mild epilepsy, has to close her eyes. They trudge along slowly forward for a half an hour before reaching the second checkpoint. A burly bouncer with face tattoos eyes them and levels a clipboard at them.

"Guys, fifty bucks. Girls, ten. Cash only."

Mahmood and Alvaro reluctantly fork over the cash as the girls pool together their own stack of tens. Alvaro can't help but think about how this cash-only rule would never work in LA, where credit cards reign supreme. The bouncer gives them a stamp on their right hands. It's of a blue cartoon rhino.

The next chamber is another long hallway, this one with muted green walls and an ornate golden finish. The room's been separated down the middle length wise by a red rope.

A gaunt man with a handlebar mustache studies the group closely from the start of the rope, saying nothing even after several of Sam's friends have offered a friendly, "Hi!"

Behind the creepy hipster gargoyle, a fact becomes clear. Undesirables, all male, have been put to the left side of the rope. This boisterous mob seethes with cologne and frustration. Many of them groan hungrily at the sight of Sam's friends.

The man points to the right side of the rope and Alvaro and Mahmood breathe easier. The man produces a little tube of paint. He colors Alvaro and Mahmood's left pinkies with a dab of neon green paint.

The rejected males on the left side of the rope jeer despairingly as the group passes them on the right. Their verbal threats are obscene and depraved, but they don't dare cross the line, because somehow they still think they might have a sliver of hope to get in. Some of them actually do if they pay exorbitant amounts of money, but even then, Diplo and all of the girls would be long gone.

Once through this room, the group comes to a narrow staircase. Each step is bigger than the next, so by the time they reach the top they have to jump slightly to advance. Through this door, they make it into the club.

Or so they thought. The club in all its glory is right in front of them, but a maze of red rope lies in front of them, through which scores of clubbers traverse. Too far to turn back, the group sets out. Mahmood goes to duck underneath a rope, but Laura grabs him and points to an array of cameras on the ceiling. They set forth more cautiously this time.

The maze leads them around the club, the whole time,

teasing them with a perfect view of the packed, pulsating dance floor. The pathway leads them away to a little enclave with a mermaid sitting on a sofa. The mermaid is beautiful, unblemished, covered in wavy red hair, and a high-quality fabric tail with glimmering scales stitched in.

"Welcome," the mermaid sings, "Who here has the most followers on Instagram?"

All eyes turn to Samantha who solemnly steps forward. The mermaid looks Sam up and down stoically, "Show me."

Once the mermaid has reviewed Samantha's opened phone, she hands it back. The mermaid presses a button hidden among the fabric of the sofa which causes the entire piece of furniture to slide back, creating a walkway into the club floor.

"Diplo shall be on in twenty," the mermaid warns, and then points at Samantha, "If you would like to meet him, be at the southwestern entrance by two thirty. No one else may come with you."

The group disperses into the club, Sam and Alvaro sticking together near the edge of the pool, Mahmood, Laura, and Kimberly at the bar. Matilda and Caroline post up in the middle of the dance floor to attract horny drink buyers which come in steadily.

Around midnight, Diplo comes on, at least according to the crowd surrounding the DJ pit. Their shouts and screams signal that the EDM artist is in the room, but there are so many people in the DJ pit that it's difficult to make out which one is actually Diplo.

Near the bar, Mahmood, Laura, and Kimberly have just

finished their second twenty-five dollar shot when an unknown hand grabs Kimberly's butt. The three furiously try to search out the culprit, but nobody's coming clean.

"Let's go outside," Laura drapes a protective arm over Kimberly, "It's too hot in here anyways."

Over by the pool, Sam and Alvaro watch the sweaty masses listen to Diplo. Sam shouts over the bursts of electronic buzz, "This place kinda sucks. Which one is Diplo?"

Alvaro screams back, "What the hell did the mermaid mean? For you to go meet Diplo?"

"It's how most musicians get laid. It's quite easy for them, really. They just ask security to get the hottest girls to go backstage. It eliminates the need for actual flirting. And it works well because girls really want to tell their friends that they got to see so and so's penis."

"Fascinating. I wonder how many STD's Diplo has."

"I'm sure his security has condoms at the ready."

"What's the most famous penis you've seen?"

"You don't want to know."

Mahmood, Laura, and Kimberly appear by Sam and Alvaro. Kimberly is sulking, "Can we go?"

"Definitely," Sam and Alvaro reply simultaneously. Alvaro adds, "Where are Matilda and Caroline?"

The five scan the entire club but can't find either of them. Out come the phones and soon the group texts blow up. *Matilda and Caro, where are you???* They wait fifteen minutes with no response, inch their way around the club once, and then snake their way to the exit.

Around one in the morning, Alvaro, Sam, Laura, Kimberly,

and Mahmood find Bernie at the same roulette table. Spectators are crowding around the table, but none dare sit. Alvaro ventures in a far chair, but the minute his butt touches the seat, Bernie growls at Alvaro.

"It's me, Alvaro! Remember?"

A glimmer of familiarity flashes across Bernie's face, and the growl evolves into a subdued gurgle. Alvaro stands, both hands up, and backs up slowly. Then he notices the tens of thousands of dollars in chips in front of Bernie.

"How much are you up!?"

Bernie burps. The croupier answers for him proudly, "About a hundred grand!"

"Holy shit!"

With assembly line precision, Bernie drops hundred-dollar chips onto individual numbers on the board. The croupier has to warn him that he's two hundred dollars away from exceeding the table maximum of five thousand. Everybody stands on their toes to get a better look. The croupier spins the ball. Bernie finishes by putting two hundred on green zero. The crowd gasps. The croupier flashes her hand over the table, "No more bets!"

The little white ball falls cleanly into green zero. The crowd explodes into applause, drawing all in the casino closer. Alvaro and Mahmood hug and kiss, Samantha high fives an old man in a walker. The croupier and the pit boss are even clapping.

Bernie just sits motionlessly as $7,000.00 is printed out on a receipt and placed in front of him. He shakes his head suddenly and everyone falls quiet.

"I want it in chips," he demands to the croupier.

The pitboss shakes his head, "You're done. Tonight, you're done."

"What would you like to do?" Laura asks Bernie. The six sit in the food court, munching on sugary delights. Most of the color has come back to Bernie's face. He's looking more like his old self, just richer.

"The strip club."

"The strip club? You just won two hundred grand, and you wanna waste it on blue balls?"

"Yes, of course!" Bernie slaps the table, "Let's go! I'll order a limo!"

The limo picks them up outside of the casino and takes them down the strip to the Sapphire Club, a sizable venue a few blocks off the Strip. None of them have done any coke this night, because they don't need to. There's some sort of primal desert energy keeping everyone wired.

Bernie struts out onto the floor of the joint like he owns the place. Sam, Alvaro, Laura, Kimberly, and Mahmood trail as his proud entourage. Dancers with fake tits and butt implants take notice and prime themselves to move in. Men in ruffled business suits close their mouths long enough to turn their heads and ogle the only clothed women in the room.

Dollar bills rain down on Charlize and Tiffany, two buxom dancers. Charlize has several dragon tattoos that accentuate her curves. Tiffany has classy piercings in every sexual organ known to human physiology. They dance in a booth surrounded by Sam and Alvaro's group who watch in joyous fascination and throw money like confetti. Early 2000s hip hop blares.

Charlize eyes Samantha curiously and sways closer until she's giving Sam a lap dance. Everybody cheers and Mahmood starts chugging Grey Goose.

"You dance around here?" Charlize asks, bouncing rhythmically on Sam.

Sam smiles and shakes her head, "I'm in the industry, though."

"Cammer?"

"Yes!"

Charlize looks over at Alvaro who grows redder than Tiffany's lips. Both Charlize and Samantha giggle.

"Y'all are on Voypure! I recognized you!"

Alvaro prays she's not going to start talking about his penis out loud. Charlize winks at him, "You've got a hot cock!"

Mahmood spews Grey Goose everywhere.

"Madre mia..."

"I'm on Voypure as well, but nowhere near as popular as y'all. We should collab!"

Samantha twitches nervously, "Maybe. What's your username?" She pulls her phone out.

"I follow your account; I'll message you on there. There's no phones allowed in here, honey. I actually lived in San Diego for half the year, but I have a condo in Studio City. We could definitely do something there."

"Okay, we'll watch your show!"

"Watch my show!? You're watching it, right now!" Charlize leaps up so both her feet are on either side of Samantha's legs then jumps up again, spreads her legs midair, and lets herself fall down onto Samantha, catching herself at the very last moment with both hands. Her naked crotch ricochets off of Samantha's quivering thighs. Laura and Kimberly squeal. Bernie showers Charlize in bills.

"You ever consider dancing?" Charlize asks after she's dismounted Samantha.

"Once or twice."

"If you think you can make a lot of money camming or on Only Fans, you haven't seen anything. I once made two hundred grand in one night!"

"You and me both, baby!" cuts in Bernie. Charlize rolls her eyes and plops in between Samantha and Alvaro. She drapes her arms over them like a veteran.

"You have to have a lot of sex with pretty gross guys. But the nights that you don't are magical. Often, guys'll just give me their Venmo and let me put in whatever I want. Plus, it's a great workout."

"Probably not as good as riding a mechanical bull!" Laura points out proudly.

Charlize frowns, "As good as riding a what!?"

"You do seem very in shape," Sam admits, admiring Charlize's thighs, "But I'm not about to dance. Alvaro and I are getting married. I've quit sugarbabying for him."

"How sweet," pours Charlize sarcastically, giving Alvaro a raised eyebrow, "And you, mister man, you gonna make her give up anything else?"

"No."

"Good. Nobody likes a needy, protective boyfriend. Especially in this line of work."

Around five in the morning, Sam, Alvaro, Kimberly, Mahmood, Laura, and Bernie crawl back into their penthouse. Caroline and Matilda are asleep while the TV blasts Selling Sunset. They're both in PJs and don't wake when Kimberly checks their pulses.

Mahmood shuffles out to the balcony with Kimberly and Laura to smoke a joint. Bernie retires to his room to calculate how much winnings he has left. Alvaro and Samantha go to their room, shut the door, and lie on the bed together, ruminating in the wisdom of Charlize.

CHAPTER 23

Samantha

I grip the steering wheel. My father, Eddie, a jumpy, bright sixty-year-old, sits in the passenger's seat. He's balding and skinny. Son of a Laotian immigrant and French expat, he murmurs epithets in three different languages as I maneuver through traffic. I never learned any words in Lao or French besides the words that mean my dad is not happy.

My mother, Elizabeth, an obese fifty-four-year-old woman, sits in the back, clutching the door and the back of Eddie's seat for dear life. She was once beautiful, but years of laziness and overeating have made her scornful of me. She never compliments me on my appearance, only snide comments meant to destroy my self-confidence.

My driving is fine. It's the usual surrounding Los Angeles drivers that are making my parents so worked up. Their hysteria is driving me nuts.

"Samantha, please slow down," Mom moans, "You're making me carsick."

"I'm going five miles below the speed limit."

My Tesla, which my mom has already complained about as being wasteful, glides north on Fairfax from Venice Boulevard. All of their luggage is stuffed in the trunk. We're on our way to some motel in Hollywood. Aunt Millie ended up bailing on my parents, claiming that they had to fumigate their place. Not sure why a fumigation needed to happen on the exact same weekend that my parents decided to visit, but I'm sure Aunt Millie came to her senses and realized what she would be getting herself into.

"The traffic here is horrible! Everybody drives like they own the road..."

A deranged homeless man with no shirt and shoes steps out into the road with unhinged confidence. My heart skips four beats and I'm forced to slam on the brakes before I commit manslaughter. The homeless man, inches away from my front bumper, doesn't even acknowledge us.

"Jesus Christ!" screams my mom, "What was he thinking?"

"He wasn't. He's probably too high to realize what he's doing."

We watch as the homeless man lurches out into the next lane, causing oncoming cars to screech to a halt. When the man is gone, I gently press the accelerator.

We pull up to the Hollywood Stars Motel. The ratty, broken-down building is behind a twelve foot tall, spike-tipped, gate. My parents look around the surrounding squalor in horror.

My dad sputters, "I thought Hollywood was supposed to be a nice place?"

"Maybe fifty years ago," I mutter, spotting two scraggly

men smoking cigarettes in plastic chairs on the other side of the street in whispering to each other about my glistening EV. I know my parents chose this place only because it was the only place in their budget range. They're used to Texas pricing. Just so I can sleep tonight and not worry about my dad getting shanked while getting ice, I decide, "I cannot let you guys stay here. We'll get you another hotel, somewhere closer to me."

"Honey, no, this place was expensive enough!"

"How much was it?"

"Sixty a night."

"No wonder. There's a nice, safe place right near my apartment. I'll pay for it."

They both burst out in protest until finally I yell over them, "Either that or you stay here!"

"Sammie," my dad puts on his condescending smile, "We've stayed in worse places. One time, in New Orleans-"

My mom cuts over Eddie, "We're your parents, we're not going to have our daughter pay for us. How much is this new place?"

A quick Google search reveals, "Two hundred twenty five per night."

"Oh."

"Can we stop at Bottega Louie on the way over? Is it on the way?" My mom must have done some Googling of her own.

As we head west, I already feel safer but more stressed.

My parents do a bad job of hiding their amazement at the hotel I put them in. When I leave, my dad's taking pictures of the minibar while my mom is inspecting the curtains to see how easily they could come off.

I arrive at my apartment and quickly consume enough THC to sedate Laura on coke. I love my parents, but they are way too much! Alvaro and I FaceTime for a bit until I can't keep my eyes open.

It's the night of my 'art show' which has involved a mad scramble of money, mass communication, and deceit. I managed to rent studio space in Culver City for a night, for over three grand. This parents visit is turning out to be a fucking nightmare for my bank account. Plus, there's been like no time to cam with Alvaro.

I sent out invitations to the show on my personal Snapchat and Instagram, telling people to bring a plus one. I want people there, but I don't want creeps coming. Laura, Matilda, Kimberly, and Caroline have all promised to bring as many people as possible. Alvaro is bringing catering and Mahmood somehow got a major discount on wine. He offered to bring bowls of weed (WTF?), but I declined. My parents do not and will never know how much I smoke.

The space is two rooms, one larger one that people enter through and can meander through to the second one, a smaller space in which there are bathrooms down a short hallway. I've gathered everything I've done and tacked it up to the walls. All of the stuff I've rushed out in the last few weeks is hidden in the backroom, lowered inconspicuously so people focus on my higher-quality work, which is more eye-level.

My palms are sweating overtime as people filter in. The turnout is actually impressive. In the first thirty minutes, there are already at least forty people here. This, of course, is made up mostly of my friends. Still, everybody is chatting, talking about my art, and asking me questions. Alvaro, as instructed, is showing minimal affection and socializing without raising any suspicions. My parents have yet to arrive.

The ratio is good, slightly more girls than guys. I'm drifting around, greeting people whose names escape me, answering questions, and keeping a watch on the door.

Much to my surprise, Mitch comes in. He's wearing a light tank top and shorts, looking very fabulous and beachy. I extract myself from a conversation and go to greet him. He smiles brightly when he sees me approaching.

"Mitch! I can't believe you're here!"

"Samantha!" He exclaims as we hug, "I saw your story. I actually live over in El Segundo now. It was, like, so close, I couldn't not come."

"Awesome, thank you! Do you want a drink or something?"

Mitch shakes his head. Now up close, I realize that his eyes are quite red. He doesn't seem high, though. His shoulders sag a little as he scans the room. He seems exhausted. He waves to Laura who flings her hand around and beams back.

"All good with you?" I probe.

"Yeah, just, uh, training, you know. Think I'll be able to try out for a field team soon."

"That's great! What else is going on?"

He juts out his lower lip, "Nothing really. This is amazing. You made all of these!?"

"Yep."

"Wow. I wish I could do something like that," he says,

pointing at a watercolor I made of a pumpkin. He stares at the pumpkin, not saying anything else. I see a little water in his eyes. Alarms in my head began blaring.

"You okay, Mitch? What's going on?"

"Nothing, really nothing! That pumpkin, it's so nice."

"Come on, let's get you something to drink," I lead him by the arm outside. Alvaro gives me a nervous glance, but I give him a quick reassuring thumbs up. I sit Mitch down on the steps, praying that my parents don't arrive at this very moment. A few people smoke cigarettes and scroll outside.

I unscrew a water bottle and hand it to Mitch who downs half of it. He looks up at me and begins sobbing. Thankfully, people near us politely stamp out their cigarettes, put their phones away, and move farther away into the parking lot or saunter back into the gallery. I squat next to Mitch as low as my dress will allow.

"Oh, Mitch. Come on, what's going on?"

"It's so unfair. He just gets away with all this stuff. And nobody stops him!"

"Who?"

"I wanted to say no, but I couldn't turn down that much! Nobody would!"

"Are you talking about Gerald? Is this about what happened in Catalina?"

"Catalina was...something. Actually, Catalina was nothing compared to what he made me do last weekend. It was beyond humiliating. Disgusting, fucking gross. He just offered me so much. It didn't feel right to turn it down."

I scoot in closer, "Tell me."

"I'm just done. I can't anymore. My baseball career is

fucking over, I'm getting too old. The only way I can survive in this goddamn city is by selling myself."

"That's not true!" though I've had the same exact thought many times, "What did Gerald do? Was it something illegal? Did he hurt you?"

I can hear people inside asking for me, but I can't leave Mitch like this. And where are my parents? They have the address. They know what time it started. I have gotten any calls or texts.

Mitch gulps, "That's the worst part. There was nothing illegal. Nobody got hurt. But there were so many people watching, laughing, recording. Kids, their parents. I'm fucking ready to leave this place. It'll come back to haunt me. I know it."

"Tell me what happened!"

Mitch stands suddenly, accidently smacking me in the head with his elbow on the way up, "I'm gonna go, this was a mistake. I'm sorry. Seeing you, coming here...doesn't bring up the best memories."

"Mitch!"

He hurries down the steps and away towards the parking lot. I take a few steps after him but remember that my parents are supposed to come any minute and that I can't abandon my own show. Mitch's beat-up Volvo careens out of the lot. My cheek feels bruised from where his elbow hit.

Alvaro is suddenly behind me. I'm not sure what he saw. He frowns, "What was that?"

"Nothing, that was Mitch. He was upset about something."

"*'Seeing you doesn't bring up the best memories...'*"

I wave my hands in the air, "It's not like that, we shared a traumatic experience."

"People are asking for you in there," Alvaro thumbs towards the door, "You hear anything from your parents yet?"

"Nothing. Ugh, fine, okay. I'm coming."

"Did he hit you? Your face is red!"

"No, Alvaro! Fucking go back inside!"

The next hour is me making up bullshit, trying to sound like I know what the hell I'm talking about when it comes to art. Really, I just like doing it, I know how to do it, but all this dumb theory and history couldn't be less interesting.

I called my mom and dad both twice, but I keep getting voicemail. My own parents are ghosting me. I can't stop thinking about Mitch. Gerald must have made him do something horrible. He seemed so distraught I told Laura to call and text him, but she says he's not responding to her either.

About an hour before closing, I get a call from my dad, which I pick up on the first ring.

"Dad! Where are you guys? Is everything okay? Did you get into an accident or something!?"

"Everything's fine, honey," he says quietly like he's not trying to disturb someone.

"Where are you?"

"My mother and I are in an Uber, sweetie. We're really, really sorry, but we're headed to the airport. Your mom isn't feeling very good."

I want to scream. I want to throw my phone against the wall. I want to intercept their car and pop all of their tires. I created this whole thing, this entire fucking circus for them. If they hadn't come, I wouldn't have spent so much money and stress on this. Now, they're leaving! All of this is fucking pointless. The thing that's making me the angriest is that I'm not surprised. I knew something like this would happen.

"Seriously?"

"I'm sorry, Sammy. I'm sure your show is going very well. We'll let you know when we land," he murmurs. He sounds genuinely apologetic. I know it's not his fault.

"Put her on the phone."

"We gotta go, Sammy. Really, don't be mad, it has nothing to do with you!"

"Dad. Put her on the phone," I take a deep breath and scream, "NOW!"

Everybody in the gallery pauses to take a look at me. I rush outside onto the steps as my mother comes onto the phone.

"Yes?"

"Why do you hate me?"

"I don't hate you. I just don't think the way you live your life out here is sustainable."

"So that's why you're ditching my show!?"

My mom clicks her tongue, flooding me with memories of disapproval, "You may be able to fool your father, but you can't fool me. I know that show was a sham. I've known for a while how you support yourself out here."

"Then why did you come all the way out here?"

"You're my daughter, Samantha. I had to make sure you're not going off the rails. You're not, but you're close. You gotta be careful. One wrong move and it's over."

"Fuck you," I can feel all my pent-up emotions gushing

up, "You're a horrible mother. Who fucking comes all the way out to visit their only daughter just to fucking gaslight them? Why the fuck would you care how I make money? You barely scrape by. Good parents are supposed to support their kids. Maybe if you spent less of your salary on junk food, you could actually move out of that shitty apartment and plan for retirement. Instead, you're gonna eat yourself into an early grave, you fat fucking bitch."

I turn to see most of my friends hovering by the doorway. I run down the steps into the parking lot. My mom is crying on the other end, staccato sniffles. There's a muffled noise and my dad hisses, "Samantha. We'll call you back."

"I'm sorry, Dad. You fucking heard her."

"That was not nice at all, Samantha. She's your mother. I'll text you when we land."

He hangs up. Alvaro and Laura appear beside me and I fall in their arms, sobbing, feeling like an utter, worthless piece of shit. The strength has gone out of my legs.

Alvaro murmurs softly, "Come on back inside. I want to buy your painting of the lobster with mittens on."

CHAPTER 24

Samantha

My feet are on Alvaro's lap. We're sitting in my apartment. We just finished up a tiring but successful cam session. At least three privates, and we gained over three hundred new followers.

We're both scrolling on our phones. I'm on Insta, he's on Reddit, I think, looking at something about soccer. My feed seems to be dominated by music festival pics. I think there's one in San Francisco this weekend. Kimberly keeps posting stories of this guy's super-realistic alien costume chain smoking Juuls.

My friend Billy has a picture of Mitch at dinner, smiling above a bowl of pesto pasta. The caption says "RIP Mitchy" and there are heart emojis everywhere. I tap through a few more stories and find a similar one with an old photo of Mitch. This time, it's him in his baseball uniform, standing on a base, probably in the middle of a game. There's no caption.

RIP Mitchy? No way...

I take my feet off of Alvaro and dial Laura who picks up after the third ring.

"Is it true?"

"About Mitch? I'm trying to find out."

"Okay, let me know."

She hangs up and I go back to investigating.

Alvaro leans over, "What's going on?"

"Remember that guy who came to my gallery show who was crying?"

"Yeah? That guy who hit you."

"He didn't hit me, that was an accident. Something happened to him. I think...I think he died. Everybody's posting photos of him."

Laura calls so I pick it up and put it on speaker phone, "Sam, he killed himself. Zara confirmed it. Apparently he OD'd on Xanax and alc."

"Oh my god. Oh my god!"

Laura says she's getting another call, so we hang up. Alvaro puts a hand on my knee, "I'm so sorry. That sucks."

"He was right there. I should have done something. I should have called somebody."

He shakes his head furiously, "This is not your fault, Sam. You can't think like that. It was probably the piece of hay that crushed the camel."

"Oh, it's definitely not my fault. But I know whose it is."

"Who?"

"Mitch was a sugarbaby, like me. We had the same client, a guy who didn't really have boundaries. A creepy old dude. When Mitch came to the art gallery, he kept talking about how Gerald, the client guy, made him do something. He didn't say what, but it must have been something insanely horrible to make Mitch kill himself. Oh my god!"

"Well, again, you don't know what drove Mitch over the ledge. It could have been growing up for a long time, or maybe he'd had some family stuff going on."

"I don't know. He seemed pretty distraught over this one thing."

"As I said, it was probably the straw that crushed the camel."

"That broke the camel's back," I correct him. My hands are shaking. I've never been so close to death before. He took his life so soon after seeing me. He was trying to confide in me, and I just let him run off. I should have followed him. I should have made sure he didn't do something irresponsible.

"Well, a good sign that you made the right decision to quit that shit. Did the client guy ever make you do anything very horrible?"

I shake my head. An idea suddenly forms in my mind, something I know I have to do now. Gerald will know what he did.

"He can't get away not knowing what he's done."

"Who?"

"Gerald."

"The client? What do you mean?"

"He's gotta pay for what he did to Mitch. We gotta make him suffer."

Alvaro spreads his fingers and puts out his hands like he's steadying himself, "What the fuck are you talking about?"

I fly up. I feel righteous energy flowing through me. I feel like I could lift a car. With one hand, I start throwing on my clothes that were strewn on the ground and the couch. With the other, I open my phone and start messaging Gerald. I ask to see him. I'm going to set up a meeting and roast this fucker.

"What are you doing?" Alvaro demands, "Who are you texting?"

"I'm gonna go confront Gerald. He needs to know what he did."

"No! No! Sam, no! That's not a good idea!"

"I'm sorry, Alvaro. I have to do this."

"What is that going to accomplish!?"

"He's just sitting out there, blissfully unaware, probably scheming to do the same shit to somebody else. If I can't put him in jail, I at least want him to suffer."

Alvaro grabs my wrist, a little bit too tightly. He releases immediately and takes a deep breath, "Don't do this. Please."

"Why are you so against me doing this!? I thought you'd be more supportive."

My phone buzzes. Gerald has resent his address and told me to come over whenever.

"Because it's pointless. The damage is done. This guy obviously enjoys embarrassing people, he's gonna get a hard on as soon as you start yelling at him!"

My flip flops are nowhere to be found, so I throw on a pair of tennis shoes without any socks. Where are my keys? Where are my goddamn keys?

"Have you seen my keys?"

"This is dumb. You just need to stay away from this dude! Obviously, he's toxic, look what happened to Mike!" he pleads.

"Mitch. His name was Mitch," I find the keys in a pocket in a jacket on the floor, "Wanna come with me?"

"No. If you go, I'm going home."

"Fine. What a great fucking financé," I spit then I storm out, making sure to slam the door behind me.

Gerald's house is in deep, deep Benedict Canyon. I'm a little scared when I arrive since my phone reception is next to nothing. I wouldn't be able to call anyone, but that doesn't matter, I'll keep my distance. Alvaro, what a fucking wimp. He should be supporting me better!

I park the Tesla on the street and march up Gerald's manicured winding front path, lined with squat palm trees, ferns, and rocks. His house is huge, three stories tall and wider than my entire apartment building. It's a gaudy design, white wooden panels with a sterile black finish. The windows are all tinted black and square, extremely cookie cutter. The boring facade gets more daunting the closer I get. I've been inside before but knowing I'm about to chew this guy's head off is making my palms sopping wet. I don't plan on going inside this time.

I ring the doorbell and wait. As I listen to the muffled echoing, it dawns on me that I don't know what I'm going to say. I didn't rehearse at all. All good, just speak from the heart. Say what you think!

Gerald answers the door in shorts. Just shorts. His milky, veiny chest makes me want to wretch. He eyes me hungrily, "Samantha! I'm glad you messaged me. What do I owe for the pleasure?"

God, even his expressions are gross. What a fucking creep.

"Did you hear about Mitch?"

He puckers his chapped, thin lins, "No. What happened?"

"He killed himself."

"Oh no," Gerald frowns slightly, as if he just heard his favorite restaurant just closed down, "That's horrible. He seemed fine the last time we saw each other."

"What did you make him do?"

"Excuse me?"

"What did you make him do? He came to me crying because of something you made him do. So what was it?"

"That's really none of your business."

"You killed him, you know that! It's your fault!"

"Now, now," Gerald puts up his hands defensively, "I know you're sad and all, you and Mitch being former lovers, but no reason to take it out on me. What Mitch and I did was between two consenting adults, you should know that better than anyone."

"Mitch and I were not former **lovers**! We only fucked because you paid us to! He was gay, Gerald. Mitch was gay. And you forced him to be with me. What the fuck did you make him do?"

"I didn't **make** him do anything! I also never **made** you do anything. I offered to pay him and he took it, same with you. You both were fully compensated."

"You're a fucking psychopath."

"I'm a psychopath? Are you sure about that?"

I want to slam his head with the door, but that would be a bad look, especially after I just accused him of being a psychopath.

"Just tell me what you did."

"You really want to know? It involved a mask, a leash, and a public park."

"You're a monster."

"I'm a guy who knows what he wants and has worked hard to be able to buy it. You all offer yourselves up so easily just for a bit of money. You wouldn't exist without me," He takes a menacing step towards me. I stumble backwards, almost off the porch, as he rants ominously, "Your generation is so goddamn lazy, expecting everything so quickly and when it doesn't go your way, you claim abuse. You never take the long road. Why work an honest job when you can post nude photos online? Because when shit hits the fan, you feel like you have the right to complain about how unfair life is, but really, you put yourself in this position. You and all these young fucking idiots."

"I'm gonna out you for the monster you are!" I roar, "You're forgetting that I have all your personal info, asshole! I know where you work, I can talk to your ex-wife, your coworkers, everybody! They will all know what kind of a pervert you are!"

Gerald chuckles, turning back inside, "Go ahead. Nobody'll see it your way."

He goes to close the door, but stops, his evil eyes bulging. He studies me from head to foot so invasively that I feel like I'm being groped, "I'll pay you to do the same."

"What?"

"I'll pay you to do what Mitch did for me."

"Go fucking die."

"Seriously. I'll pay you half a million. Five hundred grand, right now."

My vision blurs and I begin to feel nauseous. This was a mistake. Alvaro was right. I need to get back to him. I have to get out of here.

"Not enough? I'll pay you seven hundred fifty thousand if you do this. It'll be quite easy. Takes an hour. I'll pay you in cash, up front. What do you say? Can you turn that down? All you have to do is pretend to be my pet. Three quarters of a **million** for one hour of work?"

Somehow, I'm able to spin and stumble down his pathway back to my car. The stupid Tesla handle won't pop out. Gerald laughs maniacally and shouts after me, "A million dollars! I will pay you one million dollars!"

Finally, I'm in my car. Gerald's still shouting, but I can't make it out through the closed doors. I suck in air, trying to steady myself. I start the car, pulling slowly out into the tight canyon street. Thank God the Tesla does most of the work, because I can't see shit through all the tears.

CHAPTER 25

Alvaro

I still can't believe she went to go see him. I really hope she's okay. I obviously wanted to go with her but going with her would have justified her reasoning. Fuck, maybe I should have gone with her? No, I was right! There's no reason to go see him. She's just mad. Did she have a thing with this Mitch guy? Is that why she's so upset? He was quite good looking. I still think he hit her.

I'm about to go off and find her when she calls me. I can hear her crying and driving.

"Alvaro?"

"Yeah? Are you okay?"

"I'm fine," she sniffles, "I'm on my way back. You were right."

"Did you talk to him?"

"Yeah, the fucking asshole. I shouldn't have gone there."

"Well, just get back here safe. Pull over if you need to."

Somebody honks at Samantha and she mumbles something

indecipherable. She clears her throat, "Can you meet me at Shake Shack? The one on Santa Monica? I really just want a burger."

"Right now? Why don't you come home first? We can Door Dash it."

"I'm already here," she claims.

"The one right next to the Sprouts?" I grab my keys and slide on some slippers.

"Yeah."

"I'll see you soon. Don't go anywhere!"

If you've lived in Los Angeles, you know what a California rolling stop is. For those who haven't lived here, that is when a driver approaches a stop sign, presses the brake so the car slows to five miles an hour, and then accelerates past the stop sign. You don't actually stop, you slow down just enough to appear cautious and keep the ability to slam on the breaks if somebody happens to be doing the same thing in your intersection. I'm sure many people do it in other places, but we love to give a Californian name to whatever we can.

Around Samantha's apartment, there are tons of streets with four way stop signs (and practically all around the West Side) so I've become an expert roll-stopper. I'm rolling through stop signs, heading northeast to meet Samantha at Shake Shack, when a black BMW zipping down a cross street fails to slow at all and rams into my passenger door at twenty-five miles per hour.

My car's forward momentum, along with the new sideways push, causes me to spin out. I feel my tires lose control. My rear left bumper heads towards the sidewalk. I slam on the brakes which causes my tires to screech terrifyingly. I pee a little bit.

The world comes to a standstill. Everything is silent. I stare out the windshield at the deserted street in front of me. All apartment complexes, all these little boxes on top of each other. Cars line the street, more boxes. Palm trees provide little cover and sprinkle the ground with sharp, brittle leaves. Palm trees are tacky foliage if you ask me. I prefer pines.

I hear a car door open and close. A short guy with a chin strap beard and backwards baseball cap approaches my door, filming. He peers into my window, "Hey, you okay!?"

I fumble with my door. The fresh air hits me like a train. Luckily enough, I don't feel any physical pain. I'm able to get out and stand. My head is still spinning. The guy starts filming every angle of the accident.

"I called 911," he says calmly, "Just getting evidence for insurance."

"What happened?"

"You ran right out in front of me."

"I stopped at the sign. You didn't," I wave at the crushed front bumper on his car.

"Don't think so. Anyways, everybody is okay, that's what's important," He says, closing his phone after getting a shot of my back license plate, "Let's trade insurances?"

Chinga tu madre. I shake my head, "I don't have that on me, right now. Could we settle without it? I can give you my number?"

"What? We gotta do this through insurance, dude," the guy points to his front bumper, "You see what you did to my car!?"

"You did that!"

"Are you kidding me?"

"Please, man, I'll pay you in cash. What do you want?"

"Nah, fuck that. Give me your info or I'll tell the cops you're uninsured!"

Whatever happens, I cannot let the cops see my expired visa. Glen told me that Los Angeles is what they call a Sanctuary City, meaning the government won't report illegal residents, **unless** there is a crime. And I've heard plenty of stories of undocumented people getting reported by city officials. I have to figure out a way to get out of this. I can't run, because this chin-strap asshole has a picture of my license plate.

"Seriously, how much?"

Chinstrap Asshole shakes his head, scrunching his chapped lips into a tight sphincter, "Fuck you, you're going jail!"

"Asshole, you were texting! I saw you! You went right through the sign!"

"I was looking at directions!"

"So what!? You didn't even slow!"

"What kind of dumbass drives around without insurance?"

"Come on, man. Not everybody can afford to drive around in a beamer."

While the guy records me and hurls insults, I call Samantha and tell her what happened. She tells me to send a pin, which I do. She says that she's on her way. I tell her to drive carefully.

It takes a full thirty minutes for the cops to arrive, at which point Chinstrap has retreated into his front seat to pout. The cops, one stocky white woman with thick glasses and an old asian man with a crew cut, park their cruiser off to the side, turn on the lights and inspect the scene. Instinct tells me to run but obviously that would put me into a whole different world of shit.

The two officers decide to talk to Chinstrap first who exaggerates his account with wild gestures, "I'm on my way to my nephew's birthday when this dickhead runs the stop sign and tries to cut me off. I was going too fast to stop and swiped his car which spun out that way. I call you guys, like the good, taxpaying citizen that I am, and then I ask for his insurance, but he refuses to give it to me! Betting he doesn't have any! He tried to bribe me into shutting up!"

The female cop writes this down, asks a few clarifying questions about how the accident happened and then turns to me, "What happened?"

"I stopped at the sign. After making sure that nobody else was there, I go forward only to be hit by him," I jab my finger at the smushed beamer, "He didn't even slow down at the sign. I saw him on his phone."

They ask me some questions about how fast I thought Chinstrap and I were going. They tell us both to sit on the curb. Samantha's Tesla pulls up down the street and parks. She hops out and jogs towards the intersection. I see Chinstrap eyeing her curiously.

"That your girl?" he smirks.

"I don't know why you have to be such a dick about this. I could probably give you more than the repairs would cost."

"Crazy how a fucking lowlife scrub can get a girl like that."

"Que te den por culo, cabrón."

"Speak English, you're in America!"

The cops come over and ask for our driver's licenses.

Chinstrap throws his at the male cop. All three of them look at me. The female cop blinks, "Sir, your driver's license?"

"I forgot it at home."

"Passport?"

I shake my head which starts to hurt like a motherfucker.

"Ha!" Chinstrap nods triumphantly. The cops look at each other. The female cop frowns, "Okay, sir. Here's what we're going to do. Since you've failed to provide a form of identification, we're going to impound your car and take you down to the station."

"But I didn't do anything!"

"Look at my fucking car!" Chinstrap screams.

"Shut the fuck up, douchebag!"

"Go back to your own fucking piece of shit country, you fuckin wetback!"

I black out for a second. When I come to, I'm on top of Chinstrap. My fist bleeds profusely, but not as much as Chinstrap's nose. I hear Samantha screaming my name as the two cops drag me off Chinstrap who lays in the gutter, groaning in pain. They cuff me and chuck me roughly into the back seat of their cruiser. Samantha runs up, saying something, but my ears are ringing too loud to hear.

"Call Glen!" I stutter over and over. Samantha approaches the cops, but they tell her to back away. They make sure Chinstrap is okay, propping him up and checking his pupils. Another cruiser pulls up. The two original cops get into their cruiser, not saying a word to me.

"You don't understand, I didn't do anything!"

As they drive off, I twist around to watch Samantha. She stands there in the middle of the intersection, mouthing something. For the life of me, I can't make out what she's saying.

They book me for driving without a driver's license and for assault. That Chinstrap asshole should have been taken in for hate crimes, but they claim they didn't hear him say anything. Samantha and Glen arrive about an hour and a half after me. The cops sit me in the precinct on a bench on the side of the room with my hands cuffed.

Finally Glen is allowed to talk to me. They lead him over to me, keeping their distance, like I'm some rabid animal. My immigration lawyer looks burnt, more than usual, but still not as bad as we were from Carlsbad. Flakes of skin hang off his bald head and neck. He's wearing a Hawaiian shirt, cargo shorts, and flip flops. He looks like he was just at the beach.

"Are you okay?"

"I'm fucking dandy, Glen."

Glen massages his brow, "Sorry. I'm sorry."

"I'm fucked, aren't I?"

"Leave the country, Alvaro. If you don't, you'll most likely be deported and banned from re-entry."

"For how long?"

"You've been out of status for almost a year and half, right?"

"Yeah."

"Ten years," Glen sighs, "or more. Probably more because of all this."

Ten years. A decade, at least. By the time I can come back, I'll be at least forty.

"Okay," I glance over at Samantha who waves back, "What about marriage? What if I got married tomorrow?"

"I'm afraid that won't work. You're too late. You've committed a crime, Alvaro, and it'll be extremely difficult to prove this isn't a marriage of convenience. You guys haven't been dating for that long. Do you guys live together? Do you share bank accounts? Do you have anything to prove an intimate relationship?"

"There's a lot of videos and pictures of us online having sex."

Glen chokes on his own spit, "What!?"

"They probably wouldn't accept that as evidence."

"I'm not going to ask," he tsks, looking Samantha up and down quickly, "You could try to get a student visa in a few years, but I can pretty much promise that they'll deny you. With all the unlawful-"

"Yeah, okay, okay," I cut him off, "I get it. Can you ask them if I can speak with Sam?"

Glen scurries off. In a few minutes Samantha comes over and takes Glen's spot. Tears pour down her face. I want to reach out and hold her, but my hands are still cuffed. She reads my mind and hugs me. It feels wonderful. A cop shouts gruffly, "No touching!" so she pulls away. The second we break contact, my heart starts to race again.

"What's going to happen?"

"I have to leave," I choke, "Gotta go back to Mexico."

"Marrying you won't do anything?"

"Apparently not. I might be able to come back in a few years. Maybe. Probably not."

"Alvaro! This is all my fault!"

"How?"

"You were on your way to meet me! Oh, fucking shit."

"It's not your fault."

"People say that when it actually is," she moans, "I got you deported! I got my own boyfriend deported! I got my own **fiancé** deported!"

"I did this to myself, Sam! I was here illegally for over a year before we met. It was just a matter of time. You already helped me so much. You shouldn't feel sorry at all."

We sit together there for a bit, not saying anything. Thankfully, no one comes over to take her or me away. I can't believe that this is how my career, relationship, and visa all end. I have no fucking clue what I'm going to do when I get back to Tepic. My mother will be happy, at first. But I'll be miserable which will eventually turn her happiness into frustration. The past eight years were all for nothing. Funny enough, I'll probably have to start working in my uncle's restaurant, serving fat tourists and drunk locals.

I'm going to miss Samantha. We've been dating for such a short time, but it's felt like an effortless lifetime. The cuddles, the inside jokes, the excitement, the explorative sex. Not only did she give me more free time for acting, which I admit I wasted, she fully supported it, something no other ex did.

I'm going to ask her a question to which I already know the answer. I would regret it for the rest of my life if I didn't ask.

"Would you come with me to Mexico?"

Samantha stares deeply back into my eyes. I watch her envision her life with me. What does she see? Is she happy? Am I happy?

"Oh, Alvaro…"

"Just think about it. You could come live with me. We'd live with my mom for a bit, but then we could find our own place! Money goes a lot farther there than here, especially with what we make on Voypure! We could probably buy a house near the beach. I'm not exactly sure about how to get Mexican citizenship, but we can talk to a lawyer! You could become a dual citizen!"

"Okay," she says, miserable, "I'll think about it."

"Please, Sam, please."

I can tell she won't do it. She's fixated on her feet. A cop comes over to guide her away. She gives me a frightened smile. I get the sinking feeling it's the last time I'll ever see her.

The United States of America's Center for Immigration Services must really believe that I'll make my escape into the depths of their massive country, because, after my release from the West Hollywood precinct, I'm escorted by two federal officials back to my apartment. They carefully watch me pack all my stuff, while Mahmood curses them openly in Pashto. He's promised to come visit me and check in with Samantha every once in a while. I ask him to sell whatever I can't bring in the two suitcases I'm allowed and Venmo me the profits.

I wish him luck and we cry together for a bit. It's heart wrenchingly rushed. The federal douches rush me out into a van and whisk me off down Sunset towards the 405.

I sneer smugly at them through the rearview mirror, "Why the hell would you go west right now? It's so much faster to go east to get on the 101 and then take the 110. Fucking idiotas."

CHAPTER 26

Many Years Later

Samantha sits at a nicely finished dark oak bar in a classy restaurant in Puerta Vallarta, Mexico. It's her first time in this country, and so far she's loved it. She's only been to the touristy, rich parts, but they still seem vibrant and full of culture.

Mostly it reminds her of Alvaro, who she has never forgotten. How could one forget a fiancé that used to have sex with you on camera? Especially one that was forcibly deported. She sips on a mojito, imagining what the hell happened to him. He went back to Mexico and disappeared from all socials. He never responded to any of her WhatsApp messages or emails. He could be dead for all she knows.

She checks her phone for the time and glances at the bathroom where her date is taking a strangely long time. She dearly hopes he's not doing any kind of illicit drugs. He's been a little off his rocker, but of course that comes with being a celebrity.

"Samantha?"

She freezes, drink halfway up to her parted lips. In front of her stands a man, middle aged, handsome, dark hair, and a crooked smile. He's standing behind the bar with a dirty smock on.

"Alvaro!"

His hair has receded slightly, but he's still fit. He looks more mature, but still goofy and laidback, with a tuft of hair sticking up off the back left side of his head.

"I can't believe you're here!" he stutters, taking her in. She looks the same as she did twelve years ago when they last saw each other, with the exception that she's dyed her hair blonde, and she has a new nose ring. He notices she looks a little bit skinnier, but her thighs still bunch up around her waist while sitting.

She blinks as if in a dream, "This is...insane. Do you work here?"

"Yeah. Well, I own the place. Co-own, with my tío."

Samantha drags her eyes off Alvaro and scans the packed restaurant. Happy families and jubilant parties rage on, heavily involved in their own stories, their own lives.

"Seems like you're doing quite well."

"Yeah, it's actually my family's third restaurant. We have two back in Tepic."

"Wow," she restrains herself from yelling at him, throwing the drink at him for ghosting her. She sighs and grimaces. He blushes and hangs his head.

"I know, I know. I'm sorry, Samantha," he pauses, savoring the taste of her name in his mouth, "I was so sad to be gone from you and LA that seeing it from a distance but not being able to be there...It was just too much. I had to disconnect myself from it. Start to heal. It wasn't fair for you. I should have told you what I was doing. Just couldn't bear it."

"You're still an asshole."

"No argument there."

"Like, how hard is it to just send a fucking email explaining what happened?"

"You're right."

"Stop being so agreeable! You're making me look like the crazy one!"

Alvaro smiles, "We're both crazy, remember?"

Samantha huffs, unable to stay mad at that crooked smile, "Yeah..."

"What are you up to these days? Still camming?"

"Less often. Sticking to influencing mostly."

He knows this is code for sugarbabying. He nods without judgment, "Still arting?"

"Arting?"

"Is that not a word?"

"No, it's not a verb. You could say, 'making art,' but not arting."

"My English is so rustic these days."

"Rusty!"

"Por dios."

"No more 'doing acting?'"

Alvaro starts instinctively wiping down the bar, "You know, ever since I was a little kid, all I wanted to be was a movie star. When I got back to Tepic, I decided to leave those dreams and I was miserable...for a bit. I threw myself into my family business. Honestly, I'm not disappointed. I'm not racing some crazy, unreachable goal. The money's steady and good. I'm supporting my mother. It's simple."

"Any girlfriends?"

He grins, "A few. Nothing worth talking about."

That makes her exuberant but she's a master of hiding it. He quickly fixes her a new mojito and waves away her credit card, "And you? Happy?"

"I'm good, I'm great," Samantha replies too quickly. She slumps ever so slightly, "I'm making more money than I ever have. I have a mortgage on a place in Calabasas. Did some modeling in Europe last year."

"Nice! That's great!"

"Yeah, it is," she peers into the bubbly depths of her drink, "Did some film work as well."

"Really!? Like what?"

"Just some independent stuff. More of the **adult** persuasion."

"Ah, wow. That's cool. You'll have to send it to me!"

"Fuck off!"

"I'm serious! That's really cool! You should be proud, that stuff takes skill."

"Yeah, okay."

"How's whats her name? Your friend, the bull rider?"

"Laura? You don't keep in touch with Mahmood?"

Alvaro shakes his head with a big wince, "We talked for a bit after, but only for a year or so. It gets difficult with our own lives, well, you know. I'm a bad texter. What, did Laura and he have a huge breakup?"

"They got married! It was this whole big thing."

"Laura and Mahmood married each other?" Alvaro coughs up his disbelief, "When!?"

"Well the first time was like a year after you left. But then there was the whole-"

"The first time?"

Samantha finds herself actually grinning for the first time in a while, "Oh my god, so you know literally nothing. Mahmood's visa expired so it was time for him to go back to Lebanon. There was some crazy war going on, like serious shit, crazy Middle East stuff, long story short, Mahmood didn't want to leave no matter what. He tried all this stuff, his father was demanding that he come home, but finally he just paid Laura a bunch of money to marry him. It was really weird, they had a whole wedding, her grandparents got really mad that she was marrying a Muslim, all this shit happened with Alex's weed company, they had a falling out, Mahmood and Alex, I mean, not Laura and Mahmood. Anyways, after Mahmood gets the citizenship, they split up. Mahmood moved to Denver for a few years, doing something in, like, tech sales or something. Laura was in LA still until last November, Mahmood comes back to LA and they reconnect. They're getting married officially next summer. Insane."

"That's...how much did he pay her?"

"For the first time? Not sure. She doesn't give a straight answer. We all think it's northward of three hundred, but who knows. Doesn't really matter now, I guess."

"I've been so far for so long."

"It's okay. I get it."

He reaches over the bar and touches her forearm appreciatively. It sends shivers up her spine. The touch reminds her of their physical relationship, one which horny people from the internet still have documented. They both certainly do.

Alvaro points to a far wall where a solitary painting hangs, illuminated by two lamps on either side. It's a semi-crude painting of a lobster with mittens on. For some reason, it makes her think of her parents. It takes her a few seconds to realize that she was the one who drew it. She was the painter. He bought it from her at her art show so many years ago. Samantha gasps, "You still have that?!"

"Of course! Remember the art show? The one where your parents ditched you?"

"Oh Alvaro, I can't believe it. That's amazing."

"It's my favorite thing in this restaurant, since, pués, it reminds me of you."

"Thank you..."

As hard as she tries, she can't stop the tears. Years of regret and loneliness bubble up and she finds herself declaring, "I...I...All these years, all these guys, these fucked up relationships. The only time, like literally, the only time I was happy was when I was with you. I wished that we worked out, I really do. I wish you had stayed, or I had come with you here. Alvaro, nobody, not even my fucking parents ever really supported my painting...Except for you."

"Well, Samantha, why don't you-"

She shakes her head vigorously, "No, no, no! Don't ask me that again."

"Why not?"

Before she can tell him why not, a man with long black hair, a thick mustache, and extremely handsome and familiar face springs up beside her. He squeezes Samantha's lower back and plops down on the adjacent seat with the panache that only celebrities and the very rich can muster.

"Que tal, güey?" the man says amicably, "me pone un chupito de whiskey, por fa?"

"Claro," Alvaro takes a beat to process how he knows this guy. The guy hides behind his long greasy hair, like he doesn't want to be recognized, but that makes it so much more obvious. Alvaro darts a glance to Samantha who gives nothing away except a nostalgic smile. Alvaro exhales, "Diego Luna!?"

The man winces, quickly glancing around to make sure not any attention is brought on by the outburst. He musses his hair to reinforce the force field, slaps Alvaro's outstretched hand, and throws a hundred pesos over the bar.

"Si, si, soy yo. Tranqui."

"English, please?" Sam demands, crossing her arms.

"You guys are together?" Alvaro asks in awe.

"Yeah, so? He's not the first actor I've been with."

"But, hopefully, the last!" Diego Luna curtsies with a drunken swagger.

Alvaro starts hastily cleaning the surface of the bar in front of Diego, immediately unsatisfied with the current state of the establishment. To Alvaro, everything has become magnitudes dirtier now that Mexican royalty has arrived.

"Alvaro, stop!" Sam giggles.

"You should have told me you were with Diego Luna!"

Diego shushes Alvaro violently, "Basta ya con mi nombre, compadre! You want to start a riot? It's not safe here when the phones come out. Please, please. How do you two know each other?"

Both Sam and Alvaro speak at the same time, pause to let

the other go, and repeat the process over again. Diego points to Sam, "You go."

"We were **involved** many years ago."

"Involved? He was a client?"

"A partner."

Diego Luna begrudgingly gives Alvaro a fist bump, "How'd you manage that?"

"Not exactly sure. She made the first move."

"That's not true!" cries Samantha, "I never make the first move."

Alvaro wags his finger, "You wrote your number down on the receipt for me. I texted you a few days later."

"**She** gave you **her** number?" asks Diego Luna, incredulous, "You know how much I had to pay for hers?"

Alvaro shrugs, hesitantly. The movie star scratches his scalp, turning to Sam, "He left you because of the Visa, eh? I can't imagine why any sane straight man would leave you without the law on his back."

"He wanted to be an actor, funnily enough," she winks at Alvaro.

"Oh yah? Anything I've seen?" Diego inquires, yawning. Alvaro shakes his head, letting a barback scuttle behind him. Diego looks Alvaro up and down, "You got a reel?"

"Como?"

"A reel! An acting reel?"

"No," Alvaro flushes and refills Diego's whiskey, "Nothing from this decade."

"Make a tape and send it to me. I'm directing an action comedy that takes place in Mexico City," Diego Luna drawls, mixing his drink with his index finger, "I need a hitman, a trained assassin. Give me something with silent intensity, I'll push it through casting."

Alvaro asks Diego to repeat what he just said in Spanish, so he can fully grasp the offer. Samantha takes a hit from her wax pen, patiently.

"You'd do this for me?"

"Any man that can win the unpaid love of this girl, has something special going for him. What's your secret?"

"Diego Luna is asking me what my secret is," Alvaro shakes his head.

Samantha quips, "Alvaro has a knack to be in the right place at the right time. Until he's in the wrong place at the worst time."

A group of older women who have crowded the bar recognize Diego Luna. Their squeals and demands for selfies draw the entire restaurant towards the bar. The mob surges around Diego who resignedly surrenders autographs and pictures with mechanical enthusiasm.

Samantha and Alvaro flee outside onto the street. They laugh and watch through the front window as people pour into the place from the street, heeding advice from tear-struck fangirls stampeding into the place.

"Holy shit," Samantha squeezes Alvaro's shoulder, "I'm so sorry. I didn't really realize how big he was."

"Not your fault at all. He'll give us some more business, I guess," Alvaro cranes to look into his restaurant in which there's a chant of "Diego" going up, "I just hope they don't break anything. That's insane."

Samantha shrugs, "Isn't that what you wanted all that time you were in LA?"

"I had no idea."

"Still, Diego has no right to complain," she admits, "He's fucking loaded."

"What do you think of his offer? I mean, this could jumpstart my career."

"The career that was making you and would make you miserable?"

"The visa was making me miserable, not the career. I wouldn't even have to leave Mexico for this!"

"That's true."

"Hey, you're with the guy. If you think it's a bad idea, I won't do it."

"Alvaro, you need to do what you think is best. I have no clue what that is."

He wraps his fingers into her palm. She squeezes back, happy that her palm isn't sweating too much. They begin to walk down the street, away from the restaurant towards the beach. They walk in step, like nothing has changed.

"Am I crazy to consider this?"

"Of course," she coos, "You're almost as crazy as me."

Printed in the USA
CPSIA information can be obtained
at www.ICGtesting.com
LVHW040932100823
754633LV00008B/589